ANGELS FLYING SLOWLY

This Large Print Book carries the Seal of Approval of N.A.V.H.

ANGELS FLYING SLOWLY

Jill Roe

G.K. Hall & Co.
Thorndike, Maine

Copyright © 1995 by Jill Roe

All rights reserved.

Published in 1996 by arrangement with
St. Martin's Press, Inc.

G.K. Hall Large Print Paperback Collection.

The text of this Large Print edition is unabridged.
Other aspects of the book may vary from the original edition.

Set in 16 pt. News Plantin by Rick Gundberg.

Printed in the United States on permanent paper.

Library of Congress Cataloging in Publication Data

Roe, Jill (Jill Simpson)
Angels flying slowly / Jill Roe.
p. cm.
ISBN 0-7838-1820-3 (lg. print : sc)
1. Mothers and daughters — England — Fiction.
2. Catholic schools — England — Fiction. 3. Boarding
schools — England — Fiction. 4. Sisters — England —
Fiction. 5. Revenge — Fiction. 6. Large type books.
I. Title.
[PR6068.O329A82 1996]
823'.914—dc20 96-5903

For Peggy Simpson, aunt and friend

There was a pause — just long enough for
an angel to pass, flying slowly.

Ronald Firbank, 'Vainglory'

Les Sylphides always reminds me of Mother Veronica although all those years ago she wasn't Mother Veronica, of course, just my cousin Ursula.

We are standing at the head of two lines of girls in decorous net frocks while Sister Gudule does her best on the grand piano, hauled out on to the terrace for Reverend Mother General's visit. Ursula and I count the beats while we wait to lead our lines out on to the parched grass where two evenings ago we had all knelt in a rebellious line, cutting with our nail-scissors the individual, stringy stalks of grass left behind by the mower.

I hate *Les Sylphides* and I hate Ursula but we are convent girls and not allowed to hate anything, except sin, of course. But I do and know that I am wicked. Ursula knows this too.

1

1947

It was still some weeks before Ursula came, unexplained and unwanted, into our lives. We were going away to school and by the time we reached Waterloo Station to join the train for the West Country Caro's thick lisle stockings were as full of holes as a string bag. We had sat in the suburban train taking us to London, Caro rather pleased with the effect as she picked at the holes and watched little ladders run up and down her legs.

Our mother was exasperated but, determined to be gracious in front of our soon-to-be stepfather, only smiled when Caro said, 'I suppose it could have been the Harpic. I was playing with it in the lav.'

'Well, it's too late to do anything about it now. I don't know what people are going to think of you. And leave those holes alone.'

Caro was ten and I was twelve and we were going to boarding-school for the first time. We thought in our naïvety that it was just another temporary stopping-off place, and at least we were still together. In a few weeks our mother was going to be married and certainly didn't want us around while she enjoyed herself. I couldn't really remember a time when she had wanted us around and Caro and I grew up being each other's only security, two little islands in an ocean of other people's homes and other people's families. We were left in no doubt, most of the time, that we were staying under sufferance with whoever of my mother's friends would have us for a while. As we grew older nearly everyone found the two of us together too difficult to handle and Caro, although naughty, wasn't as likely as me to wake the household with screams from a nightmare or wet the bed when the fears of the day pressed in from every dark corner and kept me, terrified, in the soaking sheets.

We were still quite young when I first began to notice that the way I was treated by my mother was very different from the way she treated Caro. I became increasingly desperate to find ways of pleasing her, too young to know that nothing would ever have worked because it was nothing I did that was wrong, it was the very fact of my being that reminded her of my absent father. His big ears, his mannish hands and flat, dark hair all tormented her each time she looked at me. Caro, so pink and curly, was like her, her faults only childish, mine already at the age of seven or eight needing to be punished so that I wouldn't grow up in character like my father, even if I did look like him.

The beatings began when I was about eight. We'd been to tea with a friend of my mother's who, for some reason I found difficult to understand, seemed to like me better than my own mother did. It was near the end of the war and Caro and I, as usual, were dressed alike in home-made frocks and sandals with the toes cut out, sitting and pushing fish paste sandwiches round our plates while the sun shone and we could have been playing on the beach. Mrs Lambert said she'd heard that I was very good at ballet and would I do a little dance for them? I was overcome with embarrassment and wanted only to be left alone, hidden in my shyness. Try as my mother did to force me, I wouldn't perform and eventually ran indoors in tears.

We were walked home in silence, even Caro not being able to coax an answer from our mother, but as soon as she had closed the front door on us she reached for the clothes brush on the hallstand, saying to me, 'I'll teach you to make an exhibition of yourself, my lady. Anything to get attention with you, isn't it? And don't think you're any good at dancing, she only felt sorry for you because you're so ugly.'

The clothes brush came down on my bottom, again and again, until I was crying properly this time. Caro was white-faced, leaning on the wall behind the front door. We both knew there was nothing she could do.

'Now go to your bedroom and draw the curtains, and don't you dare read.'

I did as I was told. I always did as I was told because if my mother had come quietly into the room and found me with a book, she would have started to cry and have called me a bloody Cuthbert, just like all the other bloody Cuthberts, full of deceit. Her tears were far worse than the beatings. I knew by the time I was eight or nine that I was bad through and through and deserved my punishments but I couldn't believe that I was bad enough to make my mother cry.

The bedroom Caro and I shared was over the kitchen at the back of the house and I could tell from the sweet, sugary smell drifting upwards that my mother was cooking doughnuts; something sweet to eat was her answer to everything. I could remember sometimes hearing the evacuees from London playing in the street, when I had been an unwilling prisoner in the dark bedroom. They were thin and some of them had shaven heads but they seemed to have so much more fun than we did and because we had to refuse their invitations to join in their games of hopscotch and tag, hostility had grown up between them and us which we accepted as a fact of life. They were guttersnipes — a favourite word of my mother's — we were snobs.

Later that evening Caro slipped into our bedroom.

'I've saved my apple core for you,' she said, pulling it out of her pocket, 'it's the only thing I could hide. Sorry.'

'Oh, Caro, go away. If she finds you here we'll both be in for it.' I ate the apple core, pips and all, even chewing the stalk into hard little strips.

'It's OK. I'll say I needed a hankie and she won't be cross with me. I expect she'll let you out soon anyway, she's expecting HIM.'

We heard the front door open and close, a longish pause and then heavy footsteps up the first flight of stairs to where our shared bedroom opened off a half-landing. He came in without knocking and sat on Caro's little bed, facing me. Caro stood very still in the corner by the chest of drawers where our handkerchiefs were kept in a Black Magic box with a scarlet tassel, looking as if she was trying to disappear through the wall. I only disliked him but she hated him with a fierceness that made her ill and I knew that later on she would be sick and have a headache that would leave her weak and not fit for school tomorrow.

'Now, girlie,' he said to me, 'what have you been doing to upset your mother again?'

He had big red hands and coarse red hair and seemed to take up most of the space in our bedroom.

'She has a hard enough time bringing up you two girls on her own,' he went on, 'and you seem to go out of your way to upset her. Were you rude to her friends, Isobel? Was that it? Why don't you just do as you're told and avoid these upsets?'

I wanted to shout at him, 'You're not my father so just leave me alone. I hate you. I hate you,' but I sat silent on my bed, using all those terrifying feelings in my head to force myself not to cry again. *He* wasn't going to make me cry, ever.

He started again. 'If you'll just say you're sorry

you can come downstairs. Now come on, girlie, we could all go for a walk.'

Oh yes, I thought, then everyone could see what a happy little family we are, strolling on the beach on a summer evening.

'But I'm not sorry,' I said. He got up from the edge of the bed, his face as red as his hair.

'You really are a most unpleasant child, Isobel. You'd better stay here on your own then, we certainly don't want you with us if that's your attitude.'

He moved towards the door, gathering Caro up with him as he went, his arm too far round her shoulders.

All that summer he spent his time trying to force us to like him. He had a petrol allowance so he took us for drives in his car or picnics on the beach, when he and our mother sat together on the rocks and Caro and I were sent off to play alone. Once or twice he took Caro's hand and said, 'Come and look for shells, girlie,' and they wandered along the tideline until her small hands were full. She always came back more determined than ever to hate him. He took us to the pictures sometimes, when Caro tried desperately to sit as far away as possible from him, but by the time the thrift along the cliff tops was dry and brown and the beaches empty and returned to the local people for the winter, we still shrank from his loud voice and answered him in monosyllables.

On Caro's seventh birthday he had arrived at the back door with a puppy on a piece of rope and Caro came as near to being animated with him as she ever managed. It was a dear little brown and black thing and my mother was in a dilemma. She had six little girls in the house for a birthday party and six little girls would tell their parents just what she did about the unwanted creature in her kitchen, already making a puddle on the floor as the six little girls in their party frocks patted and played with him as if he were a doll.

When mothers and nannies had collected the six little girls and taken them home Mrs Cuthbert turned to the man and said, 'What the hell are you thinking of? I don't want a dog here and nor does Caroline. You'll have to take it back at once. It's a stupid idea.'

'Oh, look at the girlie, she loves him already. It won't be any trouble, let her keep it, Iris.' The 'girlie' did, indeed, already love the little dog but next morning when we came down, earlier than usual, there was no sign of the puppy. Caroline never asked where it was and it was never mentioned again.

Perhaps if he hadn't terrified poor little Caro so, perhaps if we hadn't both been so determined not to let him take our father's place, life would have become a bit easier for both of us. Instead, some time that autumn he stopped calling for our mother and a terrible silence came over the house. Now, the beatings with the hairbrush or wooden hanger were accompanied by my mother's tears and her choked voice saying, 'How can you be so awful to me, after all I've given up for you.'

Once, pushed beyond endurance, punished for something I hadn't done, I said to her, very quietly, 'I hate you.'

The silence was terrifying. My mother retired to bed, having sent for her own mother and I was taken into her bedroom to see what my wickedness had done and to be beaten by my grandmother this time until my bottom was covered with red, raised weals. All this time Caro was whimpering in the outside lavatory, too frightened to come out.

We were now nine and eleven and knew without doubt that our mother would be happier without us, but we had a life of our own that we managed to live, more or less secretly, in spite of her. Caro was daring and took risks that I wouldn't try and it seemed that we had made an unspoken agreement with each other that if I was punished for something she had done, and I frequently was, we would keep quiet about it and Caro would make it up to me in some other way. Whatever we were doing we always ran home as soon as we heard the noonday firing from the quarry at Newlyn but I was too afraid to take part in Caro's more adventurous outings and stood on the sidelines, watching with envy the fun she had, getting into places where we had been forbidden to go with companions we had been forbidden to see. Although she looked like an angel with her golden curls and round, pink cheeks, she was as naughty as any of the boys she played with, coming home wet and dirty or covered in paint and tar from someone's boat in the harbour. When she was caught I was sent to my room for letting my little sister get into trouble. I could have hated Caro but I didn't, I loved her and wanted to protect her.

Sometimes, though, I felt angry that I was always blamed for all our naughtiness and once I nearly succeeded in drowning Caro. We had spent an afternoon playing on the beach at Marazion, where we weren't supposed to go on our own as it was rather too far from the house, and we'd been happily swimming and digging in the sand for a long time. Eventually we got tired of beach games and I'd had enough of Caro's teasing for one afternoon. I decided to walk over to the Mount and eventually Caro followed me, as I'd known she would. I waited until the tide was coming in before we started to walk back, knowing perfectly well that Caro was a head shorter than me. We just about made it and I was sorry that we did because I thought she deserved to drown.

One of our uncles lived on a farm a few miles along the coast and when we went to stay with our cousins we would ride their hairy little ponies along the edge of the sea early in the morning when the beach was empty except for gulls quarrelling and little bobbing waders dabbling in the dying waves. We used to set up a jumping course in one of the farm fields or ride up through the gorse bushes to the top of the hill from where we could see fields and hedges and old mine chimneys spread out like a jigsaw puzzle.

At night we could see the flashes from three

lighthouses, all with their own particular pattern of light and dark. We knelt on the wide window-seat in the bedroom and watched for Tater Dhu and the Lizard to signal safety to ships at sea.

There were foxes in the fields and once we saw a vixen with three cubs playing in the moonlight where we had been picking bluebells earlier in the day. Before the bluebells, in the spring, we had come home with hands full of primroses and violets: later on spikes of purple and white fox-gloves would stand tall above the stone hedges.

In the late summer we would try to help with the harvest, tying ropes of straw around bundles of cut barley or wheat and standing three to a stook until they had been dried out in the sun and were ready to be taken into the mowey to be built into stacks and covered with a tarpaulin to keep out the rain, waiting until the threshing machine could come. We rode home on top of the cart, hot, dirty and happy.

Those were the happiest times, when we stayed on the farm and our lives seemed settled into a pattern of light and shade and when the catkins were dangling in the hedges and the cows were let out from the warmth of the winter cowsheds to eat the spring grass we were happy to know that summer was nearly here. We could wander through mounds of slimy brown wrack along the shoreline where each bare footstep sent tiny flies winging upwards or we'd try to chip pieces of fool's gold out of the rocks to make our own pirates' hoard. Our favourite beach treasures were the little pieces of coloured glass, old bottles weathered and battered by stones and the sea into dull, opaque chips. Blue, brown and green, we competed fiercely to add to our cache. There was a special place where we knew we could find cowrie shells in the coarse sand around the rocks, where shrimps swam into our nets when the tide was in. We kept a jar of cowries on the window-sill in our bedroom, counting them like misers counting money.

When we were left to our own devices Caro and I were very happy together. Quite a number of our friends were being brought up without fathers, the difference was that theirs were away in the forces while ours had taken off just before the war with the wife of a tobacconist, whom he had seen every day when he went to buy his cigarettes.

When I was sent to sit in my darkened bedroom I used to think about the times before my father went away.

When the blackberries were ripe around our grandfather's tin mine, we used to go in great groups to spend all day picking fruit. My grandfather used his walking-stick to pull down the whippy briars and he cut off each bunch of berries with a small pair of silver scissors before giving them to us to strip.

On one of these berry-picking expeditions I saw a fairy in a hedge. My father showed it to me, bright-blue wings spread out in the sunshine, but we never told anyone else. It was our secret and

I was bursting with happiness because we knew something that no one else did.

He used to take me up the road to my grandparents' house and hide behind a hedge while I surprised them by telling them I'd walked all the way on my own, before coming, laughing, up the drive to scoop me up and kiss his clever girl.

I used to like thinking about him because I knew that he would come back one day and we could go on being happy together.

Caro couldn't remember him at all, perhaps that was why she was so afraid of the string of men who trailed through our lives. Our home was made up of a mother and two little girls and we had a nanny until she decided that she should do something towards the war effort and joined the ATS. Although we knew that other people lived differently, that was the way we lived and any man who wasn't just passing through threatened to destroy our fragile world. Lots of men did pass through; Americans, Poles, Dutch, Czech, sometimes even British, came to see us and share what we had. Sometimes they slept in our little beds and Caro and I moved into the Morrison shelter which my mother had painted a pale blue and decorated with pictures cut out of a book of fairy stories.

She was proud of us in an odd way and never showed the rages that Caro and I feared so, to other people. I was the clever one, Caro the beauty and we became used to showing off to entertain her friends, each in our own way.

While we still had Nanny, our mother could come and go as she pleased but Nanny left and we were sorry because we had liked her. She told lies to keep us out of trouble and taught us to talk in a proper Cornish accent.

My father's sisters, who had moved away, came back to Cornwall for holidays in the summer to join the rest of the family, but Caro and I were so wild, so used to looking after ourselves, that our cousins were afraid of us. We led them on expeditions to the Mount or along the rocks when the tide was coming in and the aunts thought us irresponsible and dangerous. They complained to my mother, who took our side because they were bloody Cuthberts and we were hers.

There were family picnics during those holidays when sometimes twenty or more Cuthberts would meet and spend the day swimming and talking and playing endless games of cricket: Caro and I on our home ground organising games and explorations until it all got out of hand and the aunts or grandparents had to intervene. I caught murmurs of 'Isobel — discipline — what can you expect' as I sat in isolation, banished as the ringleader, until I found the courage to run and join the group which languished without me.

My mother was always delighted when I behaved badly in front of a Cuthbert but when we got home and I was still basking in naughty triumph, her mood would change to self-pity and I was perceived as the cause of it, more Cuthbert than she would ever admit.

One day of that spring we had been down to the beach in the early morning, a time that made me shiver in the coolness of a day not yet fully astir, knowing that it would be hot later on, the best kind of a day; and when we ran home late for breakfast, we turned the corner and saw a T-shaped notice standing in our front garden. It said FOR SALE. It surely couldn't mean what it said. Someone had put it there as a joke or a mistake. It wasn't a mistake: it certainly wasn't a joke. My mother had decided to move and to move to London, which we knew was so far away that it took all day on the train to get there.

Of all the things she had ever done to us this was the cruellest, because it wasn't done with any purpose in mind other than to separate us from our father's family. While we were near them her influence over us couldn't ever be complete but once there was no one to see the results of the bullying and stem the tears, once there was no one who *believed* what I said and who accepted us as two normally naughty children but who loved us for ourselves, once that had been achieved she could do with us what she liked. No one to question her lies, no one to know when we were left sobbing for her when she didn't arrive home from a little jaunt, no one to *love* us.

By the time our new life began in the dusty, dirty streets of post-war South London, buildings shored up or fallen down altogether, queues, bomb sites, noise and heat — it was the year of a record heatwave — she had spun a fantasy world that we had inhabited in rural poverty in Cornwall. She made friends with nearly everyone she met and Caro and I would have to sit and listen to stories that bore so little of the truth that it took us a long time to realise that they were about *us* at all. The ogres described by our mother were our grandparents, the skinflints and simpletons our uncles, aunts and cousins. Her new friends loved her gaiety and silly stories but Caro and I knew them for lies and ached with sadness to be back by the sea, where the white light lay over all the town and the smell of the sea was around every corner. We longed until we felt as if our hearts would break to be back in our grandparents' square granite house where our father had grown up, full of comfort and love, where we sat in the kitchen with my grandmother's fat maid reading *Picturegoer* and coveting her signed pictures of 'The Stars'.

We needed to walk with my grandfather in the kitchen garden, his walking-stick tapping our legs if we strayed too near the asparagus bed, or sit in the potting shed, eating little red apples and watching the warm Cornish rain fall on sweet peas and roses until the ship's bell outside the back door called children and gardeners back to the house.

My mother's decision to move to London was incomprehensible to us, of course, but a girl she had met during the war, called Barbara, was now married and living south of the river:

> There's so much going on here, Iris [she had written], you'd love it. Remember what it was like when the Yanks first arrived? Well there are plenty of opportunities here, if you know what I mean! Bill's working for a builder just for now but it won't be long before he has his own firm. It's all the war damage, it's going to bring in work for years and there's lots of money to be made if you know the ropes. You could find a job easily enough, the girls must be old enough to look after themselves by now and Bill can find you a little flat. We could have fun, just like the old days.
>
> PS I'm now known as Babs!!

It was on this promise of fun that we found ourselves living in two rooms of Bill's brother's house. We shared his kitchen where, in the winter, the rain trickled through the damaged roof, and his bathroom, where paralysing draughts blew through the badly fitting window frames. We, who had been used to looking out of the window on to a turquoise sea, dancing with diamonds in the summer and watching the waves roaring in, white-capped, in the gales of winter, had to make do with a little strip of grey grass and piles of builders' litter. For a long time we used to listen for the seagulls but grew used to starlings and sparrows.

That first summer London was like a cauldron. There were cracks in the earth of the gritty back garden where we could put our arms down almost to our shoulders. Everywhere seemed so filthy and dust blew and plants died. Caro and I used to go exploring the streets around our new home and I always lost my bearings but Caro nearly always knew where we were. She used to hold my hand, 'Past the Fire Station, up the hill, look for the church spire and we're home.' Neither of us was deceived into thinking it was really home and we would lie together on the mattress we shared on the floor of the bedroom, damp from the heat that seemed worse at night than during the day, listening to our mother talking and laughing next door.

Night times were best really because in the dim light we couldn't see so clearly the dingy wallpaper and odds and ends of furniture Bill's brother had used to furnish our 'flat'. We used to take it in turns to describe to each other our old home or our grandparents' house, working slowly all around the walls, over the floor, taking in pictures and books. Pipes, tobacco and walking-stick — our grandfather's; little brass letter-scales, old straw garden hat — our grandmother's. Skulls and antlers in the outer hall, tiger-skin rug, green baize door, portrait of our grandfather in his full dress uniform, attic bedrooms full of treasures.

'Big bed with copper tin of biscuits on the table. Long mirror that tilts up and down. Silver brushes and paper cone for hair. Purple wisteria all around the window.' This was our grandparents' bedroom and the thought of it was almost *too* painful. Caro always fell asleep first anyway so I could keep some of the sadness to myself without having to share it all with my sleeping sister.

We were quite used to having different 'uncles' who came and went but Bill's brother, whose name turned out to be Frank, seemed to be around all the time now. Of course it *was* his house but we could hear him in the other room of our flat most evenings, and at the weekends he organised outings for all of us. We had to be washed and tidied, clean socks on, hair brushed and ready when he called to take us on the tram to the park or 'up to Town' as my mother now called London.

He was a tall, thin man with dry skin and dry hair like coconut matting and he didn't know how to talk to children. He liked us to be quiet and well behaved. He wasn't a speculator like his brother but kept the accounts for Bill's new business, which was prospering as Babs had foreseen it would.

On one of these Sunday outings we were sitting on a bench in the park, listening to other children paddling and longing to join them, when our mother said, 'I've got a surprise for you. Guess.'

'We're going home to Cornwall,' I said.

'Don't be so *stupid*, Isobel. Think of something *really* nice that could happen.'

I had thought of something really nice so we waited and at last she said, 'Frank and I are going to be married. Isn't that lovely? Give us both a kiss, then. You are funny girls, I thought you'd be so excited.'

That night on our shared mattress even our

picture-making game didn't work. I knew Caro was crying, great drops sliding silently down her cheeks into the pillow.

'I'll never call him Daddy,' she said, 'never, ever. She can't make us. We'll just call him Frank.' So that was settled. That night I really did come near to hating my mother.

2

That interminable summer dragged on. Meat went rotten overnight because we had no fridge; milk went sour and, one day, to my horror I found the dustbin full of maggots. There was an indoor swimming-bath a short walk from the flat and we tried to find some coolness in its echoing, chlorine-smelly shelter but the word 'polio' was in the newspapers and on the wireless so we had to stop going there any more. All the same we were very busy. My mother and Frank had arranged their wedding for the beginning of October although they didn't tell me or Caro this. What they did tell us was that we were two lucky girls because we were going to be sent to boarding-school. A convent in the country where a friend of Aunty Babs had sent her daughter and she could thoroughly recommend it. My mother still believed in Babs's recommendations so we started to shop for our winter uniforms.

One navy-blue suit. One black felt hat.
One navy-blue tunic. One navy-blue raincoat.
Four Viyella blouses. One navy-blue cardigan.
Six pairs of navy knickers with elasticated legs.

Six winter vests. Six pairs lisle stockings.
Wellington boots. Outdoor shoes. Indoor shoes.
Washing kit. Mending kit.
Hockey stick and boots.
Ballet shoes and tunic — Isobel.
Navy-blue shorts. Two white Aertex blouses. Gym shoes.
Two pairs warm pyjamas. Dressing-gown. Slippers.
Six handkerchiefs.
Leather handbag.
Stationery and stamps.
One white dress for feast days.
One missal. One rosary.
Pocket money for the term.
A small tuck box. Jar of Marmite.
A small torch.
One family photograph.
Suitable clothes from home for occasional wear.
Blazer and tie.
Blankets — two
Eiderdown — one
Sheets — two pairs, white.
Pillowcases — two.
Towels — four, plain. Two facecloths.

It was just two years since the end of the war and it wasn't easy to find all the clothes we needed so we made many expeditions to Town in that sticky, hateful summer before we managed to tick the last item off this huge list. The only part I enjoyed at all was buying my ballet shoes at Anello and Davide, black leather for exercise work and pink satin points, which I was only just old enough to use.

Sometimes the days in London went well, we finished our shopping early and my mother, in high spirits, took us to a matinee. Afterwards we walked home from the bus stop, arms linked, singing the songs we had just heard, hands sticky with the juice of cherries or tiny grapes we had bought from the street barrows.

Finally we bought a trunk as all our bedding had to be brought home at the end of every school year, and a suitcase which we were going to share.

Everything, every last sock and handkerchief, had to be marked with Cash's name tapes and my mother refused to sew on any of them, so Caro and I had to do it ourselves with the thread getting greyer and more tangled as we struggled on until everything was done.

There were two items on the list which we didn't understand. One missal. One rosary. My mother said Frank would look after these and when we were packing our suitcase on the evening before we left for the start of term he gave us each a book and what looked like a necklace except that it had a cross hanging from the bottom row of beads. These, he said, were our missals and rosaries and the nuns would tell us all about them when we got to the convent so we weren't to worry. Until then we *hadn't* worried, not about the nuns anyway, but now something sinister seemed to be happening to us over which we had no control.

It was still tremendously hot at the beginning of September when we all set off together for Waterloo, Frank carrying our shared case and Caro and me in our unsuitable winter uniforms. The trunk had gone ahead of us by Carter Paterson.

The platform was crowded with girls in red and grey and navy as the train was a Special, taking us all to different schools in the West Country. There were family groups and lone parents, some girls obviously being chaperoned across London by Universal Aunts, a few brothers. Nearly everyone seemed to know everyone else, only the few new girls in their overlarge clothes hanging back from the general exchange.

My mother looked around for Babs's friend, Mrs Rainbird. It wasn't difficult to find her as she was one of only two or three women there wearing the New Look. Her pale-grey dress had a tiny waist and a full skirt that came down almost to her ankle-strap shoes. I thought she looked wonderful, prettier than anyone I'd ever seen, but I heard my mother murmur to Frank, 'Common as dirt,' at the same time as she held out her hand to Mrs Rainbird.

'My dear, how lovely to see you. Thank goodness it's the beginning of term at last. I can't *tell* you how much the girls have been looking forward to going to school with Esther.'

This was not true. We had seized on the name Esther Rainbird and had walked about chanting it in disbelief and delight for days, but looking forward to going to school with her, no.

'Loved your mother's hat,' Esther said to me later on the train. I had been deeply embarrassed by my mother's choice of clothes and looking at Esther's funny, smiling face I knew I'd met my first friend.

Two nuns were on the platform waiting for us when the train drew into the small station where we had to get off.

'Gosh, they look like Laurel and Hardy,' I said and there was a burst of laughter from the girls near me. Someone said, 'They always hunt in pairs,' and we hauled our cases out and stood wondering what to do. Laurel bustled up.

'I am Mother Patrick and this is Mother Benedict,' nodding towards Hardy. 'New girls will form a double line and come with us. Your luggage will follow you.' As we shuffled into two lines Mother Patrick's eyes skimmed over us, lingering for a moment on Caro's holey stockings. Her eyes were like blue marbles. Perhaps I imagined it but she did look as if she only just managed not to laugh. She led us at a canter from the station to the convent, Mother Benedict bringing up the rear, puffing and perspiring as she tried to keep up.

We turned in at a gate set in a high grey wall and it looked as if we were going to go straight up the drive to the front door until Mother Patrick swerved to one side, stopped and rang a bell beside a much smaller door in the wall of the main building, which was also a dingy grey. An old nun was sitting in a sort of glass box beside this door. There was a chair in it and just enough room for her to squeeze herself out and open the door for us. As we walked through it we could see that we were in a garden of sorts; there were paths and square flower beds and a covered walk running along two sides of the building. We learned to call this a cloister. At the far end of the garden was a tennis court and as we approached it Mother Patrick whirled around and held up one hand. It was bony and looked very white against her black habit.

'I am going to take you straight to your dormitory, where you will wash your hands and tidy yourselves before tea. After tea you may unpack your belongings and take a walk in the garden before supper. It is the rule here that there is no talking in the dormitories without special permission but as term doesn't start officially until tomorrow you may talk today until lights out.'

I looked round for Caro. She was ominously pale.

'Please, Mother Patrick,' I had to force my voice out, 'I think my sister is going to be sick.' She turned her hard blue eyes towards me and I noticed with revulsion that her steel-rimmed spectacles had rubbed the bridge of her nose quite raw and that there were green patches around the edge of the wound.

'What is your name, child?' She knew perfectly well what my name was because she had called it out from a list at the station.

'Isobel Cuthbert, Mother Patrick.'

'Well, Isobel Cuthbert, you will soon learn that

it takes only a little self-control to stop yourself from being sick. Offer it up for the souls in purgatory,' she said, turning to Caro.

I had no idea what she was talking about and was glad when Caro *was* suddenly sick in a flower bed. I already hated it here. The door that had closed behind us had closed out the noise of normal life, of cars and people walking together in the streets, and this grey building and grey garden were almost worse than London. How *could* my mother and Frank have sent us here. I knew I was going to cry and saw that Mother Patrick knew it too and I also saw that it didn't matter to her at all.

She whipped around once more and led us through another door into the house and along a corridor where our feet squealed on the polished floor. There was a sweet, unfamiliar smell everywhere, like the few seconds after you blow out a candle, but spicier than that. I soon came to recognise it as incense, the smell of every convent, everywhere. At a right-angled bend in the corridor there was a statue of a woman in a long white dress and a blue cape. She had a ring of stars around her head and held her arms out towards us. There was a night-light in a little blue jar in front of her and a posy of flowers. I thought she was quite pretty and kind-looking and wondered who she was.

Mother Patrick led us up a dark staircase and we came very suddenly and surprisingly on to a balcony which ran around three-quarters of a circle. Below us was an open space with coat pegs and lockers and above our heads was a glass dome which gave light to what would otherwise have been a very dark building.

Our dormitory was straight ahead and Mother Patrick walked along the lines of beds calling out a girl's name from a list she carried. Each bed was in a cubicle with wooden sides and had a curtain, now drawn back, which could be pulled across for privacy.

'Mary Clare Duffy, Patricia Meredith, Antonia Fairfax-May, Stella Lightowler, Regina da Silva, Isobel and Caroline Cuthbert.' She stopped at the end of the row and there was a cubicle with two beds in it. Two chairs, two lockers with mirrors, two sets of jug and basin. The cubicle was not quite double size and had a door in the back wall. It couldn't be divided into two singles, so sisters always shared it. Caro and I were glad to be together as we had never slept apart but that door was a bit of a nuisance as the lay teachers would use it as an escape route into the building next door, appearing without warning through our curtain, often bringing with them the other-world smell of cigarette smoke and sometimes another smell that reminded me of when we lit the Christmas pudding.

Mother Patrick continued her walk up the opposite row of beds. 'Esther Rainbird, Rosemary Williams, Deirdre Byrne, Mary Matthews, Veronica Stonor-Mitchell, Sheena Cameron and Carmel McKenna.' We each stood in the cubicle she had said was ours.

'Patricia Meredith is late and you will notice that I have omitted one cubicle. That is where I sleep. I am your Dormitory Mistress and I am a very light sleeper.' She said these last three words very slowly, looking up and down the two rows of beds. 'Silence will be kept at all times in the dormitory and once the light has been turned out you will compose yourself for sleep by crossing your arms over your chest and praying for a good death, if it should come in the night.'

Caro looked as if she was going to faint.

Mother Patrick continued, 'Esther Rainbird is your Dormitory Prefect and will maintain discipline in my absence. I trust you to obey her as you would me. You may change your underwear on Wednesday and Saturday and there is a list of bathtimes on the noticeboard in the gym. Please be in time for your bath and do not take more than your allotted twenty minutes.'

There was more.

'Your basin of water will be emptied in the sink at the far end of the dormitory and your jug refilled, in *silence*. This is not an occasion for levity.' As it turned out, it often was, but she went inexorably on, 'Each girl will attend Mass and Benediction on alternate days and this dormitory's Mass mornings are Monday, Wednesday and Friday.' It looked as if Wednesday was going to be a busy day, Mass — whatever that was — and clean underwear. 'When the bell goes you will get out of bed immediately, strip your bed, fold the bedclothes and place them on the chair at the foot of your bed. After breakfast you will make your bed and fold the counterpane up off the floor to enable the sisters to clean more easily. Esther will show you what to do.

'This school is run on the word of honour of its girls and you are trusted to do what you know is right. To disobey or to give of less than your best is to hurt Our Lady who is the mother of us all and whose example you should try to follow. If you do not get out of bed *at once* when the bell goes you will come to bed immediately after supper, in silence of course. No one will check up on you — you are *trusted* to obey the rules of the convent.'

I had already forgotten more than I could remember of what Mother Patrick had said and although I was already afraid of the little blue-eyed nun, I put my arm round Caro who looked tired to death.

Mother Patrick looked at us and I think she was going to tell Caro to stand up straight but changed her mind and said in a more normal voice, 'It's been a long day for all of you so wash your hands and come down to tea. Sister Gabriel will show you to the refectory when you are ready. Like all of you, Sister Gabriel is new to the convent so please do your best to help her.' She turned around, her black skirts flying, and left us alone.

Esther came over. 'Don't worry, it's not all so bad. Paddy's got eyes in the back of her head so don't ever try to con her and she does have favourites. Me, for instance,' she gave a huge grin, 'but she's generally fair. Did you know all the nuns have shaved heads?' We both shook ours. 'Paddy wears a night cap. If you go to the lav in the night you can see her if you squint through her curtain. Come on, we'll probably have cake today. Make the most of it, it doesn't happen very often.'

As we weren't usually allowed to talk in the dormitories we soon developed our own sign language and by leaving our curtains not quite drawn we held silent conversations with Esther and Rosemary as we could see them from our cubicle.

We struggled with the unfamiliar job next day of stripping and then making our beds. We discovered that the water in the only tap in the dormitory was cold. This wasn't a hardship now but in the winter months we had to break the ice on our jugs to be able to wash in the mornings. The only hot water we had was for our twice-weekly baths. I hated those freezing mornings. One day as we finished saying grace before breakfast Mother Patrick rang her little brass bell so we stayed standing in silence.

'Isobel Cuthbert.' My name was called in the silence. 'Have you washed properly this morning?' It was useless to lie as she always knew.

'No, Mother.'

'Then go at once and wash yourself. I am disappointed that you cannot be trusted to perform such a straightforward task.'

The whole school and Sister Gabriel watched as I left the refectory, crimson with humiliation. When I came back my porridge and tea were cold but Mother Patrick's marble eyes dared me to show any reaction and I ploughed my way through the bowl of sour greyness without a shudder. I was already beginning to learn.

That first day would have been difficult anyway but just before the mid-morning break, Sister Gabriel slipped into my classroom, whispered to Mother Clare and Mother Clare called out my name.

'Isobel, you are to go with Sister Gabriel. She will take you to the parlour where Reverend Mother is waiting to see you.'

I felt a rush of terror, knowing that I must already have broken the rules and memories of my frequent punishments at home swam in my head. Now it was all going to start again. Sister Gabriel didn't look threatening; in fact she looked very sweet. She wasn't any taller than me and had a merry little face and a turned-up mouth that looked as if it was always ready to smile. Of course that changed over the next few years as Sister Gabriel's life became remorselessly entangled with ours, but for now we were all starting our life at the convent together, so innocent and so young. Caro was waiting outside my classroom door and gave me a look that mirrored my own fears.

'Come viz me. Come.' It was the first time we'd heard Sister Gabriel's voice and I was surprised that she had a foreign accent. We passed the statue in the corridor again and were led almost back to the door where we had come in yesterday. We stopped outside another door and Sister Gabriel turned to us.

'Tidy now,' tweaking Caro's hair ribbon. 'Gut. Remember, curtsey please to Reverend Mother. Be not afraid. I wait.' She knocked on the door and gave us an encouraging nod as a voice said, 'Enter.'

The parlour was very dark with green drapes half closed over thick lace curtains. The tables and chairs shone like a bottle and the sweet smell I'd noticed yesterday was even stronger in here. There was another statue like the one in the corridor, but smaller, and a terrible picture on the wall opposite the door. I knew it was Jesus from the pictures in the books we'd used in the various Sunday Schools we'd been to in Cornwall, but this Jesus seemed to have his heart outside his chest and it was dripping blood. It was quite the most dreadful thing I'd ever seen in my life but I could hardly tear my eyes away from it.

'I see you have noticed our picture of the Sacred Heart.' The voice came from the shadows near the window and we both looked towards it. Mother Benedict was sitting next to another nun who must, I supposed, be Reverend Mother, so I nudged Caro and we both dropped an embarrassed curtsey.

'Please sit down, dear children,' she pointed to a little green velvet sofa, 'you need not be alarmed. I have wonderful news for you.' It flashed across my mind that she was going to say that our being there at all was a terrible mistake and that we were being sent home, but she went on, 'Your mother has entrusted us here at the convent to instruct you in Catholic doctrine and when you are judged to be ready, to be baptised into the one true Faith.'

I didn't understand and I knew Caro couldn't, but I didn't know what to say so I just waited.

'You know I'm sure that your mother is to be married soon and that your stepfather is a Catholic.'

I still didn't understand what Frank going to church on Sundays had to do with us.

Reverend Mother continued, 'Later on when you understand what all this means we will discuss this further if you wish but for today we will keep things simple. Your mother is a Catholic too, did you know that?'

I shook my head, Caro just sat staring at the nuns. Her fingers scratched at the green velvet seat until Mother Benedict stopped her by a tap on the wrist with the book she was holding.

'Yes, she is a Catholic too. When she married your father it was outside the Church, which was a sin but in this case also a blessing because she is able to marry your stepfather *in* the Church. It is as if the first marriage had never taken place.'

I felt as if someone had punched me very hard in the stomach. At twelve years old I knew what bastard meant. There had been American soldiers stationed near us in Cornwall and even in our little town babies had been born to girls who weren't married. I wasn't sure about all the details but I knew it was a terrible thing to be. And now Caro and I were bastards because our parents had never been married, that's what this horrible woman was saying.

'We're not bastards,' I shouted, 'we're not. And my father loves us and he'll come and take us away from here.'

Mother Benedict stood up. She was very tall and very fat and her face was red and angry. 'Stop it at once, Isobel. You are *never* to use such a word again. As you obviously need to learn self-control we shall have to teach you a lesson. For the next three days you will walk in silence around the garden, after supper until bedtime, asking forgiveness of Our Lord for having wounded Him by your disgraceful behaviour.'

Caro's mouth was twisted in a very peculiar way and I hoped that she wasn't going to be sick in the parlour.

'I think, Mother Benedict, that perhaps we might make an exception of Isobel's behaviour just this once, but you must learn, my dear child, to accept God's will.'

Mother Benedict nodded but gave me a look that said, forgiven it might be but not forgotten.

Reverend Mother took two little books off the parlour table and gave one to each of us. 'These are your catechisms and in them you will find the answers to everything you need to know for the time being about the Faith. I expect you to learn by heart the answers to the questions set for you each day, and each day you will have a period of instruction from one of our teaching nuns. I, myself, will examine you both once a week to see that you have understood those lessons.'

I was beginning to get the frightening feelings inside my head that had started when I used to be shut in my darkened bedroom. Caro was sick when she was frightened but no one could see what was happening inside me and *I* didn't understand it.

'Now I want you both to look at the picture on the wall beside the door. Look at Our Lord's closed eyes very hard and you will see them open. Walk away but keep looking at His eyes. Do you see how they follow you everywhere? I want you to remember that. In everything you do or say or think, Our Lord's eyes are on you and he knows what is in your heart and mind.'

Caro and I went and stood in front of the picture, which I hadn't noticed before. It was a drawing of the head of Christ wearing the crown of thorns and where the skin was punctured, drops of blood trickled down his cheeks into his beard. The eyes seemed closed in agony; pencil strokes like wispy clouds across the lowered lids made it difficult to focus on them but as we watched, like some frightful dream which stays with you all day bringing fear into every thought, the eyes slowly opened and gazed straight at us.

I heard Caro giggle with fear and felt her hand creep into mine as we stepped backwards towards the parlour table, which was covered with a green cloth, hairy and rough to our hands, and then sideways to the window, still keeping our gaze on those all-seeing eyes, which followed us wherever we went.

This was more frightening than I could ever have imagined. So much that I did seemed to be wrong and cause for punishment that I was gradually making a life for myself which I lived inside my head where I could think and do what I liked. If this new Lord could see even into my secrets, where could I go to be by myself now?

I thought it far worse than the picture of the Sacred Heart and, uneasy as I was, I wondered why there seemed to be so much blood about in that cool, green parlour, sweet with the smell of incense in the air.

Mother Benedict was watching us and said sharply, 'You find the Lord's suffering amusing, do you, Caroline? I can see we have a lot of work to do with you but I'm glad to see that Isobel seems to understand how every sin we commit will cause those thorns to press ever deeper into the brow of Christ.'

I looked at Mother Benedict. Her words, spoken with such relish, were making me feel as I had once when I had stayed too long in the sun. I dragged my gaze back to the picture, the eyes were concealed once more behind the cloudy lids and I looked away quickly, afraid that my gaze would be refocused and the whole horrifying charade would start again.

Reverend Mother stood up. She was tall but not as tall as Mother Benedict and her face was a waxy yellow. She had a large hooked nose and bright-grey eyes. It was the face, used to commanding obedience, that had looked out from generations of her ancestors' portraits that had once hung in long galleries of châteaux, now looted and lost. Even we could feel her powerful personality but instead of being overwhelmed by it we felt safe with her. As our weekly instructions with her progressed we learned that she never destroyed our frail confidence with sarcasm like Mother Patrick or made us feel uncomfortable by malicious innuendo like Mother Benedict. Reverend Mother was exacting in her expectation of us and gave praise and censure where it was appropriate but for the first time since I had left my grandparents in Cornwall I began to think that here was someone who, if I said something was true, would accept it as the truth.

That was still in the future, of course, and Caro and I had weeks of struggle ahead of us to learn the whole catechism by heart. We also had weeks of struggle with the disciplines of daily life in the convent. Because of our mother's disinterest in us we had become very inter-reliant and until our move to the confines of the awful London flat, had roamed all over our home territory, perfectly safe because everyone knew us and would report back to our grandparents if we stepped seriously out of line. Now, we had to conform in all outward matters to strict rules and it was agony to both of us and, for the first time, we were separated by age. Where once we had acted together for self-preservation we now had to fight some of our battles on our own.

It had been decided that the best way to integrate

us into the Catholic way of life was for us to behave as if we were already baptised with the exception of not being able to go to Communion. Until we had been accepted into the Church and had made our first confession, we sat in the pews with the other non-Catholics while everyone else went up to the altar rail.

There was so much to learn: the sacraments, feast days and fast days, the fifteen mysteries of the rosary, penance, novenas, ejaculations and indulgences, the precepts of the Church, the Stations of the Cross, the lives of the saints and above all our duty to God and love of Our Lady. We said the Angelus three times a day and everyone stopped whatever they were doing when the bell rang. It was a discipline taught us, to stop *immediately,* half-way through writing a word or brushing our hair, whatever. There were Mass and Benediction and apart from some of the prayers we said aloud during the day, everything was in Latin, learned parrot fashion for the time being. Hours of special coaching in Latin came later.

Term proceeded with our daily instruction and frequent punishments for breaches of discipline. It was the silence we found so difficult; Caro and I sharing a cubicle but not allowed to talk to each other except for some absolute necessity. I thought it was a necessity to hear what she had been doing during the day but Mother Patrick didn't seem to agree. I was still afraid of Mother Patrick but not in the same way as I was afraid of Mother Benedict's maliciousness. I decided that my own rule would be to obey Mother Patrick except where Caro was concerned. Caro and I were one unit and rules meant for other people wouldn't apply in her case. I felt a lot better when I'd decided that.

I told Esther how horrible I thought Mother Benedict was and she agreed with me. 'She cheats too,' she said, 'I hate playing croquet with her because she stands right over the ball and hides it with her skirts and then pretends she hasn't moved it.' I hated her in my head but I was already learning that to hate anyone was wrong and a sin although I found this concept too difficult to understand for the moment.

Once or twice Father Ryan came to sit in on Reverend Mother's weekly examination and it was he who was to prepare us for our baptism, first confession and First Communion. His presence inhibited me. I wasn't finding it too difficult to learn by heart all that we had to memorise and under Reverend Mother's encouragement I was learning a little confidence, but when Father Ryan took over the lesson both Caro and I withdrew from confrontation with him. He had a quick temper and little patience with us when we couldn't understand his questions, mainly because of his thick Irish accent.

'I don't understand, Isobel, why it is that you show such intelligence when answering my questions but fail so often to respond to Father Ryan's.' Reverend Mother often finished our instruction with a little talk and I longed to tell her that he reminded me of another, red-headed Irishman, who had so terrified my sister and because we had rejected *him,* my mother had wreaked vengeance on us by removing us both from everyone and everything we loved and where we had felt secure. Would Reverend Mother have understood this? I believe that even if she had done so her answer would have been the same.

'You must submit yourself to God's will for you, Isobel. If you find it difficult ask Our Lady for help, she will never refuse you.'

The emphasis on Our Lady being the mother of us all was difficult for me. She looked nice enough, judging by the statue in the main corridor, and I liked the crown of stars around her head, but I knew that with mothers appearances could be deceptive and I wasn't ready to trust her yet.

Father Ryan loved to sing and sometimes on Sunday evenings after Benediction he would sit at the piano in the gym and sing Irish ballads and love songs in his light baritone voice, while the older girls gazed at him. He was stocky and had dark-blue eyes and black hair but I thought his stubby, nicotine-stained fingers and bad teeth more than offset his handsome face.

When Mother Patrick felt the atmosphere was getting a bit too intense she would say, 'Move over now, Father, and I'll play for dancing and we can all let off steam before supper,' and she would play the 'Dashing White Sergeant' and 'Strip the Willow' until we were all out of breath and danger was averted.

We had been at the convent for four weeks and on Thursday evening when Mother Benedict had finished our daily instruction she said, 'Reverend Mother has asked me to tell you that you will be going home for the weekend. A car will take you to the station at three o'clock tomorrow afternoon and you will travel in your uniform.'

'Why are we going home, Mother?' Caro asked the question because Mother Benedict liked her, as she liked all the pink and pretty little girls.

'I believe that your mother is to be married on Saturday.' This was said in a voice of such condescension that the impact of her words was like a shower of cold water.

We were just beginning to settle down into the life of the convent and now here was another situation for us to have to adjust to. As soon as Mother Benedict let us go we went into the garden to talk about this new development. We were each making friends of our own but this was a situation where we needed to act together. We joined a group sitting on the grass behind a low hedge. Nowhere in the garden was really private and there was always at least one nun patrolling the paths, ostensibly reading her Office but with an eye always quick to see anything unseemly or immodest. Friendship between girls of different ages was especially dangerous and discouraged, sometimes even by punishment. The nuns called these 'particular friendships' and it was a discipline practised in the novitiate which had trickled through to us; the nuns saw danger for our bodies and souls everywhere. To prevent Novices from forming close friendships was to prevent the indulgence of unnatural practices, but what these were I had no idea. Just another of the growing list of things Caro and I were learning to accept without at all understanding them. Mother Bernard, who saw how I struggled with things I didn't understand, tried to help me by telling me to 'draw down a blind in your mind, Isobel, and it will be easier for you', but I couldn't and it never was.

On this evening, then, there was a group of our shared acquaintances together in the garden, who started teasing us as they always did about the amount of time we were having to spend on our own with the nuns and Father Ryan. Regina who was the only sophisticate among us said she wouldn't trust him for a minute and it was just as well we always had a chaperon. This was often little Sister Gabriel sitting in a corner with some crochet work. It was only Stella, even then, who never joined in the teasing. She would sit quietly on the edge of the group and if I looked at her, her soft little face would smile at me as if we knew a secret too private to be shared.

Even naughty, daring Patsy could see there was something wrong when we joined them because we hadn't yet learned to hide our feelings behind the mask most of us were later able to put on, behind which we could keep some secrets in our lives. Some of us, like Patsy and Caro, learned to use smiles and jokes as their disguise; Regina's was a sophisticated amusement which the nuns never managed to undermine, but for someone like me, who had a black heart, it became very difficult to find an acceptable face and it was strange in the light of what happened in our lives that Stella's sweet nature and gentle expression should have proved so beguiling to the nuns.

3

Caro and I had to go home for the wedding of course. We knew it was going to happen some time but it did seem to us that our mother and Frank could hardly wait to get us out of the way before they got married. We hardly knew him and were embarrassed by the way he stood behind her chair and let his big hands slide down over her breasts while he looked at us with a strange, triumphant expression on his face.

The weekend started badly as we had been expecting our mother to meet us and when we got through the barrier at Waterloo we couldn't see her, or Frank, or anyone we knew. The ticket collector slammed the gate on to the platform, saying cheerily, 'Well, ladies, it looks like you've been stood up,' and went off whistling. We could see the big clock and we watched the minute hand eat up three-quarters of the face while we fidgeted and became frightened. I knew that if someone didn't come soon I would wet my knickers as I couldn't leave Caro on her own and we couldn't both go, in case someone came to collect us. It was Babs who did arrive eventually, blonde hair and fox fur flying. She looked cross.

'I've got to go the Ladies, Aunty Babs, can you lend me a penny, please?'

She looked in her purse. 'Oh, you are a nuisance, Isobel, can't you wait? I haven't got a penny, you'll have to get change for a threepenny bit at the bookstall. Pick up the case, Caroline.'

We settled into Bill's car. Babs handed me a thick, brown-paper carrier-bag and a towel.

'Don't you dare let Caroline be sick in Uncle Bill's new Riley. I didn't want to fetch you in it knowing what she's like, but it seems everyone else is too busy to bother.'

She lit a cigarette and we looked out of the windows at bomb sites and building sites, all making money for a hundred Uncle Bills to buy a hundred new Rileys.

Frank's house looked different from the way it had been when we left for the country four weeks ago. Three bedrooms had been made out of our little flat and our belongings were spread through the part of the house where Frank had lived on his own. Caro and I pushed our way through what seemed to be a crowd of strangers, looking for our mother. We found her in the leaky kitchen. She had a flushed, untidy look and a glass in her hand.

'Oh, there you are at last. Where the hell have you been, and for God's sake, Isobel, go and brush your hair, it looks like rats' tails. And take your sister with you,' she called after me. Whatever we had expected, it wasn't this. She seldom kissed us but I had thought she would be as glad to see us as we were to see her.

In our bedroom the mattress had gone from the floor and in its place were two single beds. This, at least, was an improvement. There was a camp bed squeezed into the space between the foot of our beds and the wardrobe.

'It smells horrible in here, Bel.'

There was a pile of greyish underwear on the floor and I pushed it with my foot under the camp bed. I didn't want Caro to see the stains on it.

'Open the window for a bit, perhaps that'll get rid of it.'

It was a windy October day and as we pushed up the badly fitting bottom half of the sash window, the bedroom door slammed shut, making us jump.

I saw the girl reflected in the mirror on the front of the wardrobe even before I turned around to face her. She was gorgeous. Her hair was thick and wavy, not quite auburn, and her long, chocolate-brown eyes and biscuit-brown skin gave her the exotic look of a young Rita Hayworth.

'I'm Ursula,' she said, 'and those are my grandmother's clothes you're kicking. I'm sleeping in the spare room, except that it isn't any more, it's *my* room now. Didn't they tell you?' She laughed just a little. Just enough. Caro was kneeling on her bed and asked,

'Didn't tell us what?'

'That I'm going to live here and go to school with you. My grandmother is Frank and Bill's aunt.' She said impatiently, 'Aunt Thora, you must have heard of *her*.'

We had, of course. Rather we had overheard whispers, conversations that stopped when we came into the room. Aunt Thora was bringing up her daughter's child, abandoned overnight when Bet, who had always had a taste for the unusual, ran away with a black American soldier. Why hadn't my mother and Frank told us about Ursula? Why should she have a bedroom to herself while Caro and I were squashed into this little room, full of her grandmother's smell and dirty clothes.

Ursula looked at us in our thick uniforms and said, 'You'd better change, hadn't you? Why don't you put on those,' and she nodded to the two matching dresses hanging behind the door. 'Hurry up and we'll go downstairs together.'

Caro and I changed into the pretty silk dresses meant for us to wear to the wedding tomorrow, not even noticing how the long eyes watched us. There was a scene of course; my fault for wanting to draw attention to myself as usual, and as we were sent back upstairs to put on old skirts and jumpers, I heard Ursula saying, 'I tried to stop Bel, Aunty Iris, but she insisted on wearing it today.'

In that one moment, the time it took for a stranger to align herself with my mother and against me, I knew that Ursula was an enemy.

Babs, as she now insisted on being called, was my mother's Matron-of-Honour of course. Caro and I, wearing the silk dresses again, sat with our grandmother in the front pew while Ursula sat across the aisle with Frank's Aunt Thora. Ursula wore a pale-yellow wool dress with a full skirt and Peter Pan collar. She looked lovely and although our dresses were pretty, with a pattern like dozens of small seed packets scattered on the material, it was obvious that we were children and Ursula was a young woman. At least we knew where to genuflect and when to make the sign of the cross by this time but the Nuptial Mass seemed to last for hours.

The reception was in the local Sports Club. Where old men played bowls in the summer and met to drink in the winter, our mother started her life as Mrs Rocastle. She looked happy and very pretty in a suit of cream shantung and a hat covered all over with bunches of lily of the valley. I loved her so much it was like a pain every time I looked at her and I didn't want Frank to take her away from us.

Whenever I looked at my mother and Frank, it seemed that Ursula was there, not exactly *with* them, but always close, always ready to fetch a cigarette or my mother's handbag, compliant and charming in her grown-up yellow dress, and it was to Ursula that my mother handed her bouquet for safekeeping, the delicate, bright flowers I so wanted to hold; some small part of my mother to keep alive until she was safely back from her honeymoon and waiting at home for us to come back to her in the holidays. I sensed Ursula watching me, and when I went to the cloakroom the flowers were in a jug of water by the basin and I determined to take them home with me and not to let Ursula have them.

As the afternoon grew dark little groups of guests sat around with cups of tea, talking and laughing, and I noticed that my mother and Frank had disappeared. I felt panic starting to hammer in my chest. They had already gone on their honeymoon without saying goodbye and I ran from room to room feeling tears burning in my eyes. Mrs Rainbird caught my arm as I rushed past her.

'It's all right, Isobel, they haven't left yet, they've just gone to change into something warmer to travel in. You didn't think they'd leave without saying goodbye, did you? Come on, poppet, come and sit by me and tell me all about that old convent of yours. Esther tells me that you're very clever and that you dance like a dream. Is that right? What do you think of Mother Paddy then? Old dragon, isn't she.'

As I sat by her, her growly voice punctuated by little laughs gradually calmed me, although tears were still waiting to spill down my cheeks. She held my sticky hand.

'What's the matter, poppet? Frank's a kind man, you know, he'll look after you, just give him a bit of time to get used to you, that's all.'

Oh! kind, ugly Mrs Rainbird in her absurd long dress. I wanted to put my head in her lap and let the convent and Ursula and all the painful things I couldn't understand float away on her laughter. I wanted to tell her that I missed my father but that I wasn't allowed to mention him any more. She went on talking to me and I was almost all right again — until I saw my mother and Frank getting into the big black Humber that was taking them to the station.

My mother looked around, calling, 'Caroline, Isobel, where are you, come and kiss us goodbye. Be good girls now and we'll see you soon.' She hugged us both and Frank kissed us on the cheek. As my mother was looking around her, Ursula pushed her way through the crowd of people near the car, carrying my mother's bouquet. She held it out towards her.

'I'm so sorry, Aunty Iris, I can't imagine what's happened to them, they were all right when I put them in the cloakroom.' She turned to me and said clearly, 'You were in there just now, Isobel, did you notice anything?'

The broken trumpets of cream and pink freesias dangled from crushed stems, fern leaves torn and tattered, all held in a dishevelled bunch in Ursula's hands. Five minutes ago the flowers had been perfect and now my mother thought that I had destroyed them. She took the flowers from Ursula and pushed them into my hands with a little laugh, water dripping on to my new silk dress.

'Here you are, Isobel, you wanted them and now you've got them,' and she and my new stepfather were gone in a shower of confetti.

I ran down the path after the car, tears streaming down my face and shouting, 'Take us with you, please don't leave us alone, please, please.'

Mr Rainbird caught me before I ran into the road and held me tight while I sobbed my fear into his grey waistcoat. Ursula stood and watched me, an odd look on her face. It was almost sympathetic but it was gone as soon as I saw it.

Caro took the broken flowers from me and threw them on to a pile of rotting grass mowings and we sat together on a bench outside the clubhouse, shivering in our silk dresses as it grew cold. We both knew that nothing would ever be the same again and I think we were both beginning to realise that things were going to get worse. We didn't know how long Ursula had been living in our home but we could both see quite clearly, without being able to understand why, that she was already an established part of our new family and that in future we would be even further removed from our mother's attention.

The wedding guests were leaving, lights from cars quartering the bowling green and voices calling goodbye. We seemed to have been forgotten as we sat at the edge of the unnaturally smooth grass, now dark and shadowy and cold. I didn't want to go back to Frank's empty house, to have to spend another night listening to Ursula's grandmother, Aunt Thora as we had been told to call her, turning and snoring in Caro's bed, so close to me that if I put out my arm, I could touch her. Caro was sleeping in the camp bed and I was afraid to talk to her in case Aunt Thora heard us.

'Do you think we should go in, Bel? I don't

think anyone really cares *where* we are, do you?' Caro sounded as if she were going to cry and I remembered that she was still only little and that I was responsible for her.

'We'll go in in a minute, but I want to tell you something first.'

She looked at me and even in the dim light I could see that her face was pale.

'I know what it is, you don't have to tell me. *I* know that Ursula smashed up Mummy's flowers; I saw her do it but I was too scared to say anything. I'm sorry, Bel.'

'Doesn't matter, they wouldn't believe us anyway. Come on or they might really forget us and leave us here all night.'

If we had both been younger perhaps we wouldn't have seen so clearly that our mother and Frank and Ursula were now a family and that Caro and I were the interlopers. More than ever now, all we had was each other and I was determined that Ursula would never take Caro away from me as she was already succeeding in doing with my mother.

The far end of the garden where it abutted the church was where the nuns spent their recreation hour in fine weather. Reverend Mother Peter and Mother Bernard were walking around a rectangular flower bed, hands tucked into their sleeves, their veils blowing out behind them in the brisk October wind.

Mother Bernard was the oldest nun at Stella

Maris. She walked slowly, swaying slightly from side to side as if her body, hidden in the folds of her habit, was top-heavy. Her eyes were faded almost to yellow and there were a few soft white hairs on her chin. She had entered the convent a year after leaving school and the world outside was less a memory than something of which she was reminded when her brothers brought their children and later on their grandchildren to see her. She had never had any regrets about her own life and was gentle and good and she was Reverend Mother's friend and mentor.

'You're worried about the Cuthbert girls, Mother Peter?'

'We seemed to be making progress with them, Mother, but their weekend at home —' her voice trailed off. 'Mother Patrick tells me that little Caroline was sick again last night and Isobel seems afraid of her own shadow.'

The older nun had taught generations of girls in over sixty years in the convent. She had helped many bewildered children to find a place of their own, not always in the Church but, she liked to think, in the love of God. It had never occurred to her that it was *her* love which had turned around a sad young life, for she had achieved in the service of God only what she saw as her duty to Him in the place to which He had called her. Mother Bernard knew unhappiness when she saw it and in Isobel Cuthbert there was a depth of unhappiness as great as any she had encountered.

'Perhaps, Mother Peter, we should allow them

a little relaxation this week. We haven't enough time to give them a complete break from their instruction but if you feel you could take an extra lesson this week and I myself take one, we could give Mother Benedict a rest as well. I think they would all benefit.'

The two nuns continued their walk in a perfect understanding.

Ursula was nearly two years older than me so we didn't share a dormitory but she was put into the same class. It was supposed to be just for a while until she caught up but we stayed together and shared lessons for the next five years. I don't think she was lazy, as Mother Benedict insisted, I think she was really not very bright, although I was sure she could do whatever she wanted, if she wanted it enough.

No, Ursula's talents lay in the way she dealt with people. It didn't take me long to realise that she never disagreed with anyone. A small smile, a slight hesitation was enough. Usually she said whatever the other person wanted to hear and perhaps it was only because I was so obsessed with her that I could see her doing it, as her conversations and confidences were generally confidential. She managed to convey to whoever she was with that they were important to her but she always stood slightly aloof and the more she did, the greater was the clamour for her presence.

The impression she gave was of intelligence and stability. I was sure, though, that her stillness and reserve covered nothing more than a void, and I couldn't understand why no one else seemed to be able to see it too. She quickly became a favourite with the lay staff. Ursula was the one always ready to run errands or to volunteer for extra tasks, tasks given to me as an aid to helping me to submit my will to the greater good, copying out pages of plainsong so that there were enough sheets of music to go round, which I did with ill grace, or hearing the catechism of the youngest girls. If the garden needed to be weeded, Ursula would give up her free time on Saturday and work alongside the little sisters until they insisted that she stop, charming them, as she charmed so many with the implied flattery and her smile, for her smile was very appealing and one of her greatest weapons.

She seemed to do all these things out of goodness of heart but eventually we began to notice that the nuns knew when we were planning a diversion, or who had broken the strictest rule and gone out of bounds, or who had smuggled letters out with a day girl, but Ursula had the enviable gift of being absent from the site of trouble. It wasn't that she wasn't involved but she was never *there* when the account was called. She smiled and was deemed to be good and I could do worse than follow her example, according to Mother Benedict.

Mother Benedict. There, I'm sure, was the answer to why Ursula was so seldom called to account. Mother Benedict was Reverend Mother's deputy, tall and broad and with a round, red face that always seemed to be wet with perspiration.

Her glaucous eyes looked as if they were swimming in unshed tears and her damp, red mouth was so painfully discontented that I tried never to look at it.

She seemed always on the point of erupting into violence and her voice was loud and emphatic, as if she should be calling dogs to heel, not teaching children obedience. I was terribly afraid of her, for those wet blue eyes missed none of my faults, but Ursula seemed to find some perverse satisfaction in pleasing her, in drawing her sarcasm almost as if she were practising for something in the future. If Ursula was liked at all it was for her ability to coax Mother Benedict out of a dangerous mood, and although I tried to see how she did it I was too young to understand what lay behind the game they played, and was just glad of the respite that Ursula's almost flirtatious way of talking to her afforded me.

One very strange thing happened towards the end of her first term at the convent. Ursula's mother, the runaway Bet, sent her a dress from America where she was now living with a small-part actor. It was a soft, thin material and Bet had chosen pink and cream which showed off Ursula's unusual colouring beautifully. On most Saturday evenings we were allowed to wear clothes from home so Ursula put on her new dress to show us. It wasn't really warm enough for a wintry England as it was sleeveless and she hadn't intended to keep it on, but before she could take it off Mother Patrick saw her and grasped her by the arm and made her stand at the top of the passage which divided the two rows of beds in the dormitory. This in itself was unusual as the nuns tried never actually to touch us at all. Mother Patrick's eyes were flashing blue ice and her bony fingers dug into Ursula's arm.

'Girls, I want you all to see this.'

We pulled back our curtains and stood outside our cubicles to see what Mother Patrick was talking about.

'What do you think of Ursula Hosier's dress, girls? Is it pretty?' We murmured assent because it was very pretty, prettier than anything any of us had.

'I see. You *all* think it's pretty do you? Well I am ashamed of you. Ashamed that girls of your age could think that something is pretty when it is so immodest and an occasion of sin to anyone who looks at it.'

We were all silent with astonishment and Mother Patrick pulled Ursula by the arm and took her around every dormitory, where everyone was changing for the evening. It was the one time I ever felt truly and deeply sorry for my cousin and as I waited to tell her so, I saw Sister Gabriel in a dark corner of the corridor and as Ursula passed her, with her head held high and no expression at all on her face, Sister Gabriel put out her hand and touched Ursula on her bare arm. Ursula hesitated for only a second and in the look that passed between them were sown the seeds of the tragedy that was to touch all our lives.

4

Caro and I were to be baptised into the Church towards the end of the winter term and Mother Clare told us we would need white dresses and white veils. Usually we all wore black veils for chapel, held in place by a ring of black elastic. On the evening before a feast day we would find a white veil and a ring of white elastic on our beds. The convent would find us each a special veil for our First Holy Communion, said Mother Clare, but we were to write home to ask for a suitable dress each. I didn't think my mother would be at all pleased about this. Although a best white dress was part of the uniform, we had come to school without them, dismissed as an unnecessary extravagance, and nothing had been said when Caro and I had to wear our Sunday suits instead. Now, however, we *had* to have dresses and I wrote home, explaining why.

I was relieved when a parcel arrived, so big it could only be the dresses. Letters and packages were put out for us to open at break but parcels had to be opened with the Mother Infirmarian watching. Most parcels were tuck, of course, and Mother Sylvester would stand with her head on one side, watching us unwrap our parcels and as soon as she saw that they had sweets in them she would say, 'Something for the poor, please, something for the poor,' and hold out her grey, wrinkly hand.

I always hoped I wouldn't be ill and sent to the Sanatorium as the thought of those old, cold hands touching me made my flesh creep. For someone like Stella Lightowler a handful of sweets or one or two bars of chocolate didn't mean very much, but to Caro and me even a small contribution meant there was little left for us. I resented those poor who took part of our meagre rations and I wondered who they were.

The nuns themselves used envelopes which they turned inside out and reglued. They didn't make us do that but before we could unpack our dresses we had carefully to unknot the string from our parcel and fold the paper so it could be used again and even then we had to wait for Mother Clare, who was in charge of making sure that we were suitably dressed for our great occasion.

We were very excited and pulled the first dress out of the box. It was too small for me, obviously Caro's. Thin white wool with long sleeves which ended in a little ruffle, tucks down the front of the bodice and a wide sash. It was perfect. Thank goodness, I thought, and lifted mine out happily.

It was made of white satin with an overskirt of spotted net. It had puffed sleeves and a deep flounce at the hem, threaded with more satin ribbon, and a sweetheart neckline. Even Mother

Clare, usually so quiet and kind, couldn't stop herself from saying, 'Oh, Isobel. Oh dear.'

I dropped the awful dress back into the box. Surely they wouldn't make me wear it.

Caro said, 'I won't wear mine, Bel, not if you've got to wear that one.'

Mother Clare picked up the box.

'Well now, we'll have none of that, Caroline, but I think I know what we can do. I know that Stella has a dress that she's nearly grown out of and I'm sure she won't mind lending it to you and if I alter it a bit, it'll look just right.'

Dear Stella, who had so much of everything. The most pocket money, the biggest birthday cake, the newest clothes and even a little box-like portable radio, which we all coveted. I felt hot with shame, like one of Mother Sylvester's poor, but I had no choice. A telephone call to Mrs Lightowler, the discreet delivery of one of Stella's old dresses, Mother Clare altering and fitting, and I had my baptismal dress. If Stella recognised her dress she never gave the slightest indication of it.

We didn't go home for half-term, of course, as our mother and Frank would be getting back from their honeymoon at about the same time and didn't want us there while they settled in. There were always a handful of girls left at school for half-term, usually they had parents who lived abroad and they only went home for the long summer holidays, flying off to Africa or India or China on their own. Mrs Lightowler and the Merediths always used to invite any of Stella's and Patsy's friends who were left behind but everyone wanted an invitation from Mary Clare as she had three handsome brothers whose half-terms often coincided with ours. Jerome and Con were older than Mary Clare and Cormac just a year younger. The very Irishness of the Duffys' names would have been recommendation enough for Mother Patrick. It was her one blind spot and she seemed to lose her usually highly developed critical faculties when confronted by anyone from her old home, accepting them at face value.

She wasn't wrong though in her assessment of the Duffys. Mary Clare's father was a solicitor and her bubbly, unconventional mother, in her former un-Duffy days, had been an actress. They were both cradle Catholics and lived a few miles outside the town in a square golden house which was dry and warm and full of colour.

Mary Clare and Patsy had been friends since they were first put on ponies for the leading rein classes at local horse shows but Patsy's home, although similar to Mary Clare's, always felt cold and the food was rather bizarre. Mrs Meredith would have been more interested in her children if they had been horses. She spent all her time riding or in the stables and her interest in horses included the owner of the nearest thing the county had to a stately home, whose show hunters she coveted almost as much as she lusted after him. If we stayed at the Merediths' we were as likely to dine off fish and chips from a mobile van as pheasant from Sir Neville's coverts. Mr Meredith was the senior partner in the town's veterinary practice and their house was full of old dogs and their stables full of new horses.

Another local family could occasionally be prevailed upon to take in the half-term orphans and this was the Fairfax-Mays. Antonia of the not-quite-pretty face and shocking stories was to become one of my closest friends, tied together by an understanding of the love and fear each of us had of our mother. Later on, as we grew up, I stayed often with Antonia while Caro usually went to Patsy's, for this first half-term was not an exception as we thought; we never once, in six years, went home for half-term.

I loved Antonia's house. She lived with her grandmother in a huge, crumbling grey castle of a place where moss and green slime crept down the back walls and where most of the rooms were too damp and too big. We wandered from room to room, dancing and shouting and opening cupboards to find piles of mouldering clothes which we wore to our indoor picnics in the echoing rooms. It was a house full of books although the library had been abandoned when rain came through the roof. Lady Blanche had just moved all the books into a dry room and they were piled like precarious Alps all over the floor.

There was a portrait of Antonia's mother, Inez, in the dining room and I could see that she was beautiful. At that time Inez was married to her third husband, none of whom had been Antonia's father and sometimes Antonia and I would pore over old copies of the *Tatler* and the *Field* trying to decide which of the middle-aged men it might possibly be.

Antonia was rather inclined towards a Duke and there *was* something in her long face with its sharp cheekbones and her sandy-coloured hair that did, indeed, resemble the owner of thousands of Scottish acres whom we saw pictured with his dogs or, occasionally, with his plain wife. I thought it might be a Brazilian playboy, rather fashionable at that time, or one of the handsome soldiers who rode in the British Show Jumping team, but as Inez herself had never been quite sure who had fathered Antonia and was so dismayed at the long, pale baby that she had left Antonia with her own mother and gone off to France with a photographer, we knew that our search was in vain.

Leaving Antonia with her grandmother was the best thing that Inez could have done for her daughter and although Lady Blanche was a defiant agnostic, she had sent Antonia to the convent because it was the nearest decent school that wasn't awkward if the fees were sometimes rather late.

Antonia herself seemed to suffer no unease about her disputed paternity and found it almost alluring to wonder which of her mother's many lovers was responsible for her being. I was shocked but thrilled to be allied to such wickedness.

I think in the beginning it was only because Mother Bernard felt sorry for me when there was nowhere else to go that I was allowed to stay with Antonia, because she was not a Catholic and, even worse than that, Lady Fairfax-May had been well known between the wars as a campaigner for birth control for the working classes. Some of the books piled in the old billiard room had been written by her and Antonia and I had read all about intercourse and reproduction long before Reverend Mother gave us all instruction on the Sixth Commandment.

Antonia's grandmother had always answered her questions when she asked them, and in a matter of fact way, so it was Antonia who told me what incest meant and explained how someone as old and horrible as Neville de Maide could be having an *affaire* with Patsy's mother. She said that Mr Meredith didn't mind because he had lots of mistresses himself.

I was shocked too, and upset, to think of my mother and Frank doing some of the things Antonia showed me in her grandmother's books and once, discussing breastfeeding while we ate our lunch, I began to feel very uncomfortable.

'You're being a bore, Antonia,' Lady Blanche said, rescuing me, 'get on with your chop or I'll give it to the dogs.'

Lady Blanche took me in to Mass on Sundays and we didn't have meat on Fridays, but mostly she left Antonia and me to do whatever we wanted. Occasionally she took us over to Patsy's to ride, when I tried to avoid Mrs Meredith as my new knowledge made me shy of her, and sometimes into Bath, driving her shabby old car faster than I'd ever been driven before.

Antonia and her grandmother lived together very companionably, with Lady Blanche just occasionally having to sell a picture or a brooch to pay the school fees. The house was gently disintegrating around them and only Inez's old nanny and Lady Blanche's even older gardener still lived and worked there, as much a part of the family as Antonia herself. Sometimes it seemed to me that Antonia was much older than her grandmother.

The older girls were given a special talk when they reached the Upper IVth and the fact that Reverend Mother herself took a special instruction class every year for all the girls in their first senior year shows the importance she attached to the Sixth Commandment. Caro and I were to have our instruction on our own and as question 209 in the catechism grew nearer, I grew more and more apprehensive. We did know what adultery was but didn't see what it had to do with us.

Modesty was something we'd hardly even heard of before coming to the convent but it seemed to pervade our lives now. It had been impressed on us on that unforgettable evening that Ursula's dress had been immodest because it was wrong to expose our bare shoulders. We had to struggle to dress and undress and even to wash with a dressing-gown draped over our shoulders so that no glimpse of our bare bodies would cause others to sin. Mother Patrick told us it was wrong and self-indulgent to enjoy a bath and that it was better to wash sitting upright and to get out of the water as quickly as possible. It seemed very odd to Caro and me because we had been used all our lives to family beach parties where everyone wore bathing costumes and the children ran around naked, and we didn't at all understand what Mother Patrick called 'sins of the flesh'.

We sat, Caro and I, facing Reverend Mother as she asked us, 'What does the Sixth Commandment forbid, Caroline?'

'The Sixth Commandment forbids all sins of impurity with another's wife or husband.'

'Does the Sixth Commandment forbid whatever is contrary to holy purity, Isobel?'

'The Sixth Commandment forbids whatever is contrary to holy purity in looks, words, or actions.'

I could feel my face beginning to burn with embarrassment because I now understood why Reverend Mother thought this particular instruction so important. I thought of my discussions with Antonia and hoped that I could keep my thoughts hidden from the nun's probing eyes.

'Are immodest' — that word again — 'plays and dances forbidden by the Sixth Commandment, Isobel?'

'Immodest plays and dances are forbidden by the Sixth Commandment, and it is sinful to look at them.'

'The last question to Caroline. Does the Sixth Commandment forbid immodest songs, books and pictures?'

'The Sixth Commandment forbids immodest songs, books and pictures, because they are most dangerous to the soul, and lead to mortal sin.'

Reverend Mother closed her catechism, folded her hands into the sleeves of her habit and settled in her chair. She sat upright with her back not touching the back of the chair.

'You both seem to be learning your lessons well and I think it is time that we discussed the nature of sin, particularly sins of the flesh. Put your hands down, Isobel, and look at me, please.'

No escape by trying to shield my face, she would see written on it every sin I had ever committed.

Reverend Mother continued, 'When we were studying the Creed you learned that there are two kinds of sin. What are they, Caroline?'

'Original sin and actual sin, Reverend Mother.'

'And, Isobel, how is actual sin divided?'

'Into mortal sin and venial sin, Reverend Mother.'

'Good. Good. Now, today we are going to start thinking about the sacrament of Penance which you are approaching and the sins you will want to confess. In particular I want to talk to you about the sin it is easy for a young woman to fall into, as you are both at an age when you should be aware of how easily sins of the flesh can be committed.' She stopped, and looking at me, asked, 'Are you a full woman yet, Isobel?'

I knew what she meant, of course, as I had seen Mother Sylvester carrying packages covered with a white cloth into the senior girls' dormitories and, once, I'd seen her slipping a paper parcel into Esther's locker. There was a box in her office with a slit in the top like a money-box and the older girls sometimes wrote their names on a slip of paper and posted it into the box.

'No, not yet, Reverend Mother,' I said, feeling the hot blushes spreading up my neck to my face. My mother had given me a sanitary belt and a confused and hurried explanation of what it was for but it seemed quite wrong to sit opposite a nun and expect *her* to understand about periods and what to do about them.

She went on. 'You are both approaching the age when you must be on your guard at all times against temptation. The sins against purity and chastity are among the worst sins you can commit and if you die with a mortal sin on your soul — what happens, Caroline?'

'They who die in m-mortal sin will go to hell for a-all eternity.' Caro was beginning to stammer, something that seemed to have started now that she wasn't sick quite so often.

'You have learnt to bow to each nun as you pass her and to curtsey to me. Why do you do that, do you think?'

Caro said nothing and although I knew it was the wrong answer I said, 'I suppose it's just a rule.'

'No, Isobel. It is because you are acknowledging the Holy Ghost in all of us. You do not bow to *us,* you are bowing to the Holy Ghost *in* us. All our bodies are the temples of the Holy Ghost and you must always remember that. You have to keep your body clean and free from sin as the Holy Ghost dwells within you.

'Our Lady should be your model. She was born free from sin so that she could become the Immaculate Mother of God. When you feel tempted to sin you should make the sign of the cross on your heart and pray for Our Lord to help you to resist.'

I tried to look sideways at Caro to see if she had understood any of this, because I knew that I hadn't. We had been taught such a lot about sin that sometimes it seemed that just about everything we ever did was a sin of some kind. Mother Benedict had several times told us that even the smallest sin that we committed was another thorn pressed into the brow of our suffering Saviour and that by disobedience to God's will we were daily crucifying Him again. It was a terrible burden to bear, continually trying not to sin, and I was beginning to confuse what was sin and what was not. I understood that as I was wicked I should have to work terribly hard to save myself from hell, but I couldn't really believe that my little sister was bad as well. I could understand that it was wrong to tell lies or to steal something but I didn't understand about being pure, or what one did not to be pure. I thought about asking Reverend Mother but decided I would rather ask Regina as she seemed to know a lot about things that puzzled me.

I was a bit afraid of Regina; she seemed to be able to see right through you and know what you were trying to hide rather than what you were actually saying. If she liked you it was all right but if she didn't, she would mock you and drag your secrets out to be paraded for everyone to laugh at. She seemed so *old* compared with most of us and you had to be very careful with her. Even Mother Patrick's disapproval didn't seem to worry her. For some reason she hated Ursula almost as much as I did and I think it was only for this reason that she was so nice to me, for we had little else in common.

It was funny really because I always thought that Ursula and Regina looked rather alike although I knew that Regina's father was Portuguese. They both had coffee-coloured skin and dark eyes and their rounded womanly shape, even at thirteen, made them look much older than the rest of us. They seemed to share, too, some secret that none of us knew.

On Saturday afternoons when we were allowed to wear clothes we had brought from home, Regina wore tight skirts and silver bracelets and shoes with Louis heels. I knew that she was lazy and untruthful but she was very funny and shrugged her shoulders and muttered in Portuguese under her breath if she was caught talking when we were on our honour to be silent or when Mother Patrick described her dancing as 'immodest'.

Apart from swimming, she played every game so badly that we all conspired with her to enable her to say she felt unwell as often as she could get away with it. I knew that she kept cigarettes hidden in her writing case and she had shown me lipstick and powder in her handbag.

The nuns tried to alert her to the dangers for

a pretty Catholic girl living the cosmopolitan life which would be hers, and she listened compliantly enough and then mocked them as soon as their backs were turned: no threat seemed to frighten her, no punishment subdue her.

At first I had found her mockery difficult to deal with but became grateful for her protection, for Regina was the one person whom Ursula seemed wary of.

I was watching Ursula one Sunday evening when Father Ryan was singing 'The Black Velvet Band' and 'The Snowy-Breasted Pearl'. Her long, chocolaty eyes were fixed on his face and her mouth was slightly open and, I don't know why, I felt uncomfortable, as if I was eavesdropping on a conversation I wasn't meant to overhear, when suddenly Regina walked up to Ursula and pinched her hard on the top of her leg. I don't think anyone else saw her do it but Ursula turned slightly and gave her such a look of hostility that I was glad it wasn't me she was looking at. As Regina turned, she caught my eye and raised her hand towards her mouth, just enough for me to know she was saying, 'Keep quiet.' Ursula moved away from the piano and we soon started to dance to 'Sir Roger de Coverley' and I forgot what I'd seen.

I didn't think about it again until long, long afterwards and I wondered then if that had been the beginning of it all and that Regina, brought up in a world of sophisticated laxness, saw what it took me so long to realise, that Ursula's calculated enticements were beginning to draw Father Ryan into a morass of deceit and hypocrisy from which tragedy could be the only outcome.

5

Caro and I each had to choose the name of a saint to be used for our baptism. Mother Bernard gave us a list of preferred Catholic names and for a few days we called each other Concepta and Fidelma, which we thought very funny. We knew one of us would have to use Theresa as St Theresa of Lisieux, the Little Flower as she was known, was often quoted as an example of ideal girlhood. Privately I thought she sounded both selfish and feeble and was determined not to be allied to her by name. Caro said that she didn't mind so I said I'd have Bernadette, who was the other favourite of the nuns. I would have preferred Matthew or John but when I asked why the nuns took men's names and I wasn't allowed to, I was told that it wasn't something I should be bothering about and to clear such distracting thoughts out of my mind.

Our mother and Frank were coming down for the weekend, of course, as the celebrations would last for two days. On the Saturday we would be received into the Church and immediately afterwards we would make our first confession. On Sunday we would make our First Holy Communion. I didn't know how I was to stay sinless from Saturday evening to Sunday morning but I knew I had to try. I didn't think the opportunity for mortal sin would present itself, but every breath might lead to venial sin and it had been impressed on us for weeks that we had to be in a state of grace for our First Communion. What if I wilfully concealed a serious sin in confession? How serious did that sin have to be to constitute sacrilege? What if Father Ryan refused absolution? I was more frightened than I had ever been in my life and there was no one at all I could turn to for comfort. It was already obvious to me that Mother Benedict and even Mother Patrick had two standards of behaviour so how were Caro and I to know where we crossed the line from naughtiness to sin.

Reverend Mother said it would be helpful to write down a list of everything we needed to confess and in our prayer books were some suggestions that might help us.

No real difficulties with 'My duties towards God' — they would start once we were baptised, but the list of opportunities for sin under the headings 'My duties towards others' and 'My duties towards myself' filled a page and a half and I knew I was guilty of all of them.

Have I been disobedient? Yes.
Have I been wilfully unkind? Yes.
Have I been spiteful or jealous? Yes. Yes.
Have I been in a temper? Have I listened to

conversations that were not my business? Oh, yes.

Do I think myself better than others? I don't *think* so but I might as well confess it, as I expect I do.

Have I been vain? Have I been greedy? Have I done anything against purity or modesty in looks, reading, films, thoughts, conversations, either alone or with others? *Yes. Yes. Yes.*

My list grew longer as I realised I had committed every sin suggested in my *Children's Sunday Missal*, and with every new sin I discovered, the conviction grew that Father Ryan would find it difficult to give me a severe enough penance to make up for twelve years of wickedness.

Every time I thought of having to go into that darkened box and tell someone else how evil I was, I felt as if my heart was choking me, my chest being squeezed until I had to struggle to breathe.

It was no good kind Mother Clare telling us that Father Ryan wouldn't think it was me or Caro — how could he think otherwise when we were the only two going to confession that day.

All the beatings and the banishments tangled in my mind and I knew they were as nothing compared to what Father Ryan would have to give me. I imagined the worst penance I could, and thought of the humiliation of everyone watching me having to say the Stations of the Cross, crawling around the church on my knees.

Caro and I were allowed to have dinner with our mother and Frank when they arrived from London. Ursula had to come as well, of course, but I knew Ursula well enough by this time to get a perverse enjoyment from watching her please my parents. She said the things that were in *my* head but which I knew better than to say aloud, and my mother actually laughed and teasingly told her she was a naughty girl. Frank became almost jolly under her blandishments and, watching her, I didn't understand what she was doing, because she didn't appear to be doing anything other than being agreeable to her uncle and his new wife, but I did wonder why my parents, like so many others, seemed to *want* Ursula's approval.

As it was a Friday we had to choose the steamed cod but to my consternation my mother ordered the roast beef for herself. I knew I should have kept quiet but I was afraid for her, that she was committing a sin, so I blurted out,

'But it's Friday, Mummy, you can't have meat.'

'Who says I can't have meat if I want it?'

'Well, Catholics can't have meat on Friday. It's one of the things we've learnt, and you're a Catholic so you can't have meat.'

Caro sat very still, looking at her plate, while Ursula stared straight at my mother.

'I see. Same old Isobel. Three months at the convent and you know better than anyone else what I can and can't do. Fish on Fridays is all nonsense anyway and I shall eat what I like. And

I don't want to be told what to do by you, Miss Knowall. You still think you're cleverer than anyone else, don't you?'

The expression on Ursula's face didn't change at all during this little speech but Frank laughed and said, 'Oh, come on, Iris, don't let's have any bad feeling today,' and turning to me, 'I don't want to hear you speak to your mother like that again, Isobel. Do you understand me?'

I nodded and my mother gave Frank a look full of scorn. It was the last time she spoke to me that evening, not even a 'goodnight' when we had all been walked back to the front door of the convent.

Caro hadn't been stammering when we'd left home three months ago and now, as she said, 'G-G-Goodnight M-M-Mummy,' my mother straightened up and said, 'What's this nonsense you've started, Caroline? I'm not having this M-M-M business all the time. Stop it at once and talk properly.'

Something else had happened during that dinner, that left me feeling shaky and afraid. We were all looking at the menu and there was a silence. Ursula pulled a piece of paper out of her pocket and passed it to me,

'I think this is yours, Isobel. I found it in the corridor and forgot to give it to you before. I'm terribly sorry but I read it before I realised what it was.'

She handed me my list of sins, completed ready for tomorrow. She looked straight at me with that odd, blank look she sometimes affected but I knew that she remembered every last thing she had read. I also knew that it had been inside my missal, marking the page at Examination of Conscience, which I had left in my locker and there was no way at all it could have been on the floor of the corridor. I pushed the scrap of paper into my pocket feeling as if I was going to be sick and hating that softly smiling face, even though she was now lying for me.

'Oh, it's nothing really, Aunty Iris, just Isobel's prep. list, but she'd be in trouble if she lost it. It's lucky I found it.'

That night as we lay in our little iron beds I heard Caro whispering, 'Are you awake, Bel?'

'Yes, but be quiet, Caro. Paddy'll hear us.' Caro got out of her bed and crept over to mine.

'I'm frightened, Bel. I don't want to be a Catholic. Why do we have to?'

'I'm not sure. Something about Mummy not being able to marry Frank if we don't. I don't want to either. It's not fair is it, no one ever asked us what *we* wanted.'

'Perhaps we could just pretend and then it wouldn't count.'

I thought of the eyes of the picture in the parlour, seeing right into our souls.

'God would know we were pretending, but I'm frightened too. I don't think I can *not* sin all the time and I'm so afraid I'll go to hell.' Caro put her arm across me and I went on, 'You know that piece of paper Ursula gave me at dinner?'

Caro whispered, 'Yes.'

'It was my confession list for tomorrow. She *stole* it out of my missal and she's read it.'

'I hate her, Bel. Do you know what I saw her doing? She was looking in Mother Patrick's locker and when she saw me she said she'd tell Paddy that's what *I* was doing, if I ever told anyone. She makes me afraid of her sometimes.'

'She told Mummy a lie tonight too, but no one ever seems to think *she's* doing anything wrong.'

'Well, *we* know, but I don't suppose that counts much. Do you remember how she spoiled Mummy's flowers at the wedding and let you get into trouble for it? I think she's just jealous of us because we've got each other and Mummy and *her* mother doesn't want her.'

The curtain moved and Mother Patrick stood just outside our cubicle. I waited for the storm to break but she said quite gently, 'Get back into your own bed please, Caroline. Try and sleep now so you will be refreshed for your wonderful day tomorrow. God bless you,' and she went away as quietly as she had come.

I thought about what Caro had said and decided that my little sister was sometimes very clever and saw things very simply.

Some of the nuns in the convents where we went to play netball and hockey matches wore large wooden rosaries hanging from their waist and warning of their approach was always signalled by a muffled clicking as the beads knocked against each other. Our nuns, however, moved silently on soft-soled shoes and many a sentence was left unfinished when a dark shadow suddenly loomed over us. Esther had been right about Mother Patrick though; she could be frighteningly scathing but she was generally fair and sometimes her blue eyes danced with laughter and her voice would soften, the Irish girlhood bubbling through the convent's careful vowels.

When we went down to breakfast the next morning we saw that our napkin rings had been moved to the same table and our places in the refectory were marked by a coloured fan of holy pictures around our plates. The day of our reception into the Church was being treated as a feast day and there were warm, home-made sweet rolls and real butter for breakfast. We were excused the usual walk around the bleak winter garden so that we could have a last talk with Reverend Mother before we had to dress.

She didn't need to tell us to ask Our Lady for help, I had been praying all morning to everyone I could think of to stop Caro from being sick. She was very pale and quiet, as if she had just understood that the reprieve which she was sure would come was now undeniably too late.

Each of us had to have a sponsor and I had wanted Esther or Antonia but as neither was a Catholic Mother Benedict suggested, of course, that I would probably like to choose Ursula and Caro perhaps Mary Clare. I was apprehensive about the way Caro was just agreeing to whatever was suggested, she had always gone her own way but now she just said that Mary Clare would be all right. I think she was pretending that none of it was happening and that it didn't really involve her, Caroline, at all.

I certainly wasn't going to choose Ursula and, afraid as I was of Mother Benedict, I was determined to have Stella. When I asked Stella, her eyes opened very wide. She looked as if she wanted to kiss or hug me but we knew that would be a sin so she held my hand and said,

'Oh, Isobel, of course I will. It's a great honour and I'd be proud to be your sponsor.'

She looked so pleased that I knew I'd done the right thing but Mother Benedict's reaction was to say, 'Well, if you must, I suppose it will do but I do think Ursula would have been better, she has such dignity.'

The white dresses were laid out on our beds and once we had struggled into them Mother Clare and Sister Gabriel appeared to make sure we were tidy. It began to feel like a party and Caro cheered up a bit. She looked very sweet and I knew that even in my borrowed dress, Mother Clare had made me look just as pretty. New white hair ribbons had appeared beside the dresses and even our soft indoor shoes had been polished for us.

Caro and I, with our sponsors, were to go into church first, then the choir and then everyone else. As we passed Ursula she said, just loudly enough for everyone around us to hear,

'Good luck, you two. You look wizard and don't worry about the dress, Bel, you can hardly see where Mother Clare let the hem down, honestly.'

I heard Stella's 'Horrible pig' as we walked on and I tried to put Ursula's maliciousness out of my mind. It wasn't my fault that her mother had all but abandoned her: my difficulties with my own mother were hard enough for me and I didn't understand then that to Ursula I was the object of envy, for she would have preferred all the unwelcome attention I got from my mother to being ignored by her own.

Our mother and Frank were sitting near the font and I was afraid to look at her, I was so worried that she would ask me out loud in church where the dress was that she had sent me. In the next few minutes our lives would be changed for ever and all I could think about was my dress. I supposed I should have to confess to vanity and pride as well now.

Father Ryan was wearing the parish's best vestments of white satin encrusted with gold embroidery and the church was full of incense and big Easter candles which smelled of beeswax. The choir filed in singing the Lourdes hymn, 'Ave, Ave, Ave Maria', and High Mass began.

We were old enough to make our own promises to renounce 'the devil and all his works and pomps' and Isobel Bernadette and Caroline Theresa became members of the Catholic and Apostolic Church, for ever and ever. Amen. We never used the names again.

Everyone, from Reverend Mother to the kitchen sisters whom we saw very rarely, except in chapel, was beaming with happiness. Sister Paul and Sister Bridget who cleaned the dormitories and whom we often had to dodge in the corridors as they moved along behind a wide broom, catching the dust with a handful of scattered damp tea-leaves, waited outside the nuns' chapel to smile and say, 'God bless you, God bless you.'

There were tiny home-made biscuits and coffee waiting in the parlour for us; Sister Gabriel handing round the thin little cups, which had been standing on a tray covered by a cloth of snowy whiteness with S M — Stella Maris — embroidered on each corner.

I saw Frank put his hand to his pocket to pull out his cigarettes and Reverend Mother almost imperceptibly nodded to Sister Gabriel, who put an ashtray on the table in front of him. Mother Bernard had told us that ladies didn't smoke but that gentlemen often liked a good cigar, and I suppose that Players Navy Cut was the next best thing.

Reverend Mother and Mother Bernard, of course, took nothing but sat in the window-seats while we nibbled at sugary fingers and drank our weak coffee. I could hear the ticking of the parlour clock where a little girl in a golden swing moved in time to the passing seconds. The Sacred Heart watched us, gradually becoming obscured as the smoke from Frank's cigarettes rose in blue spirals.

I was finding it difficult to swallow because my mother still hadn't mentioned my dress, although she had stared hard at me when we all sat down. I knew she wouldn't say anything in front of the nuns but she wouldn't let it pass, of that I was sure.

'It was a wonderful service, Reverend Mother. The Catholics always do these things so well, don't you think?'

'I'm glad you think so, Mrs Rocastle. We are so *very* happy to have helped in bringing two new souls to God. We have been very privileged.'

Mother Bernard added, 'Isobel and Caroline have proved to be good, industrious children, Mrs Rocastle, you must be very pleased with them.'

Our mother looked at us as if she had forgotten why we were all there, drinking coffee in the dim, green parlour.

'Well, Caroline perhaps, but I wouldn't describe Isobel as "good", unless she's changed a great deal.'

'Oh, indeed. I believe that Isobel is going to be an asset to the school, Mrs Rocastle.'

If I hadn't thought her incapable of it, I would have thought Mother Bernard was angry.

'Isobel is older than most of the children we prepare for baptism and has, perhaps, found it more difficult to accept some of the Church's teachings, but by the grace of God and a great deal of hard work on *her* part, she has the potential to become a devout Catholic, and perhaps even — well, it's enough to say we are very pleased with her.'

My mother stared through the window at the leafless trees and grey wall separating us from the rest of the town. She bit her lip in the way she always did when she had something to say but knew she would be defeated by an adversary. This usually meant she would round on me as soon as we were alone, but somehow I knew it wouldn't happen today. She never mentioned the dress, either then or ever.

When Sister Gabriel had collected the coffee cups and the starched white napkins, she left us, and Reverend Mother turned to Mother Bernard, who gave her two little blue bags, stretching down into the bottom of her deep, nun's pockets to find them.

'Isobel, Caroline, these are for you to remind you of the most important day of your life.'

She handed each of us a Miraculous Medal on a gold chain.

'I want you to wear them and when you are tempted to sin, for the devil will renew his efforts now, pray to Our Lady for help. Perhaps we could all join together in a prayer to Our Lady now.'

She and Mother Bernard folded their hands into their sleeves and bowed their heads. Caro and I knelt down and Frank quickly stubbed out his third cigarette.

> 'Hail, holy Queen, mother of mercy; hail our life, our sweetness, and our hope! To you do we cry, poor banished children of Eve; to you do we send up our sighs, mourning and weeping in this vale of tears. Turn then, most gracious advocate, your eyes of mercy towards us; and after this our exile, show unto

us the blessed fruit of your womb, Jesus. O clement, O loving, O sweet Virgin Mary. Pray for us, O holy Mother of God.'

'That we may be made worthy of the promises of Christ. Amen,' we replied.

When we had finished our prayer the two nuns stood up. I wanted to throw my arms around Mother Bernard but all I could do was to thank her. Looking into her oddly faded brown eyes, I knew she understood everything I couldn't say and for the first and only time she touched my hand.

'God bless you, dear children.'

We curtsied and they were gone.

'Thank goodness that's over,' said my mother, Frank adding, 'One down and one to go.' He gave his rather nervous laugh and put a hand on our shoulders.

'I'm very pleased, you know, very pleased indeed.'

My mother looked at our Miraculous Medals. 'I don't suppose they're real gold, do you, Frank? Still, they're quite pretty. Aren't you going to put them on? We'd better go or they'll have us going to confession as well and that will never do.' She looked at me for a minute.

'You could have taken those hideous glasses off just for today, Isobel, then you wouldn't have looked quite so dreadful. I don't understand why you should have to wear them at all when I've always been able to see perfectly well. I suppose you think they make you look clever but you know what they say, "men never make passes at girls who wear glasses".'

She turned at the door and I thought she might be going to say something more, perhaps that she was proud of the way we had behaved, but she just smoothed down her skirt and she and Frank went out together. Back to the world of gin and tonic and roast beef on Fridays, beyond the grey wall that surrounded us. It didn't seem to matter quite so much any more.

In the afternoon Mother Benedict came to fetch us and took us to the chapel. Several nuns were already kneeling in the dimmed light, their faces hidden by their veils. The Choir Nuns, who taught us, wore bonnets of starched linen with a goffered frill around their faces. Their bonnets were freshly laundered for Sunday mornings, becoming wider and softer-looking as the week wore on, but on Sunday mornings they would be driven to ease the pricking and smarting on their skin by lifting the edges slightly with their fingers. The lay sisters, who did all the domestic work in the convent, wore only a half-bonnet, unfrilled but stiff with starch. Over these they all wore a black veil, the front folded back on itself, which they pulled forward to hide their faces when they were praying. They all crossed their arms and tucked their hands into the wide sleeves of their habits when they were walking or reading, as if those hands might be tempted to do something untoward of their own volition if they weren't confined. The kitchen sisters always went to Communion after Reverend

Mother but before everyone else so that they could leave chapel early to go and make breakfast. As they passed, a strong smell of greasy fat wafted along with them, caught permanently in the folds of their long black skirts.

A few people from the parish were scattered in the main church, waiting to go to confession but only Caro and I were in the chapel with the nuns. Father Ryan came in and shut himself into one of the two wooden boxes along the side wall. Mother Benedict touched me on the shoulder and I reassured myself that the list of sins was in my missal.

'Bless me, Father, for I have sinned. This is my first confession —'

I felt curiously calm once it was over but there was a tingle of excitement running through my mind, that hadn't been there before. I understood that however weak I might be, however much I sinned, there *was* hope — Hell's Jaws had retreated a pace or two. The fact that I was still as wicked as I had ever been meant that every confession was a trial of endurance. Fear of non-absolution and the ever waiting public humiliation of a visible penance never receded but, at last, I understood that God was able to forgive me, even if compassion was scarcer in those I most longed to please.

As soon as we left the chapel I hurried to the lavatory, tore my list into little pieces and flushed them away. I felt so elated at having coped with the apprehensions of the last few weeks that I didn't even mind that Ursula's place had been laid, alongside Stella and Mary Clare, Rosemary, Regina and Patsy, at our tea-table. As it was so special a day we were obviously going to have Feast Day Cakes, and once the bread and jam had been cleared away a happy hum preceded the advent of six nuns, each carrying a pink and white gateau, which they placed in front of the prefect of each table. Mother Patrick rang her brass bell.

'I think you all recognise the importance of this day to Isobel and Caroline, and after all the solemnities come the treats.' She smiled and went on, 'First, a very big "thank you" to Sister Lucia who has worked so hard on these beautiful cakes.' We all clapped and little Sister Lucia blushed and nodded her head once or twice before hurrying back towards the kitchen.

'You will be excused Preparation tonight as you are to have a Film Show in the gym.' She pronounced it 'Fill-um' and her cheeks became quite pink. 'Now perhaps, Isobel and Caroline, you would like to cut the first slice of cake.'

Together we held the long kitchen knife, as if we were Bride and Groom, and it slid softly through the layers of cream and sponge, and everyone clapped again. Mother Patrick allowed the happy chattering to grow much louder than usual before ringing her bell again.

'I shall ask Ursula, as a member of Isobel and Caroline's family, to say Grace for us tonight. Please, Ursula.'

We lifted our chairs silently under the tables,

always mindful of a Saturday evening not long before when the sound of chair legs scraping on the polished floor had brought half an hour of silent punishment, picking up our chairs, moving them and putting them down, over and over again. Most of us were self-conscious about saying Grace in front of the whole school, and rushed or muttered the words, but Ursula stood quite composedly until everyone stopped fidgeting, and then said loudly and clearly:

'We give thee thanks, O Lord, for these thy gifts which we have received from thy bounty, through Christ Our Lord. Amen.'

As we filed out of the refectory, taking advantage of the day's unusualness to talk on our way to the film show, she put her arm round my shoulders and said, 'I'm *so* glad for you, Bel. It's the most wonderful thing in the world to be a Catholic and now I feel happy that we're *really* cousins and we'll be the best of friends, won't we?'

She hugged me and I might have believed her if I hadn't seen her reflection in the long glass over the serving table looking straight at Sister Gabriel as she spoke. I saw the colour rise in the young nun's cheeks and I saw Ursula's smile.

Rin Tin Tin was followed by *The Thirty-Nine Steps*. In Mother Patrick's opinion the dog was a great deal more suitable than seeing Madeleine Carroll taking off her stockings. The sisters slipped quietly into the back row of chairs and slipped quietly out again before the end to put out buns and jugs of cocoa for us.

I'd hardly had a chance to talk to Caro alone all day and had to wait until we were changing for bed, when I whispered, 'I feel funny, almost glad, now that it's over. Are you OK?'

'I'm OK but I don't want to talk about it. You may feel glad, Bel, but I shan't ever forgive any of them. They can't see what's in my head and I shall just go on as before but they won't be able to tell, will they? And as soon as I leave this place I shall stop even pretending. Goodnight, Bel,' and she turned her back on me and fell instantly asleep.

I'd never heard Caro talk like that before. We often disagreed about things and occasionally fought fiercely, but this disinclination to discuss something was so unexpected. It seemed final, somehow, like the nuns' dismissal of an awkward question:

'Please, Mother, what is a womb?'

'A womb is something to do with Our Lady, Isobel, and does not concern you. Get on with your work, please.'

I was too tired to stay awake for long, puzzling over my sister's behaviour but I think I knew even then that something had changed, some balance had shifted and we were no longer fighting a mutual enemy but would pursue our individual daemons more and more as time went by.

When we woke next morning I hardly thought of what Caro had said but sometimes during the day her words came back to me and I felt apprehension tightening in my chest.

Our freshly ironed white dresses were hanging

on the cubicle rail and with them were two long soft veils. After the previous day's excitements, our First Communion was a quiet affair. However, instead of taking our usual places in the nuns' chapel, the whole school sat in the main church, full of parishioners for the early Mass. Our mother and stepfather were there, of course, and after breakfast they called to take us out for lunch before they went back to London on the afternoon train.

I hoped we could be alone with them for once but when we went to change into our Sunday suits, Ursula came too. I could feel anger and resentment building up inside me. Why did she *always* have to be around. I wanted to tell her that she wasn't welcome and to stay away from us, but I knew what a terrible sin it was to feel like that so soon after Communion. By the time we were all three ready I could hardly bring myself to talk to her, and she knew it. She always knew it. She looked at me with a strange expression in those huge brown eyes, so dark you could hardly see where the pupil sat in the chocolaty iris. Her mouth was soft and pink, almost as if she wore lipstick, and it pouted just slightly over her beautiful white teeth.

'I'm sorry, Bel. I know you don't want me to come and I did try to get out of it but Aunty Iris asked for me specially. She's so sweet, isn't she, and so funny. You *are* lucky to have her as a mother. I hardly ever see mine, you know, so couldn't you share yours with me?'

'Just shut up, Ursula, and don't call me Bel,

only my sister calls me that.'

'Well, we're like sisters really, aren't we, living together and everything? Why don't you like me, Bel? What have I done to upset you?'

'Well, for a start, you stole my confession list out of my missal, and you tell lies and you hang over Father Ryan as if you're a film star, and then Paddy's cross with everyone. And I know something else you've done.'

The more I spoke, the more I wanted to hurt her and I just managed to stop myself from telling her what Caro had told me. Suddenly, she put out her hand and touched the golden Miraculous Medal that Reverend Mother had given me yesterday. It made me jump as I was momentarily afraid that she was going to hit me. I should have known better, of course. That wasn't her way.

'That's pretty, Bel. Can I wear it?'

'Of course you can't. I only got it yesterday and Reverend Mother says we're to wear them all the time.'

At lunch in the rather dreary hotel my parents favoured, Ursula told my mother and stepfather how much I had wanted to give her my Miraculous Medal but that I was afraid that Reverend Mother would be upset if I did.

'Isobel's so kind, Uncle Frank,' she said, those brown eyes gazing into his, 'but I suppose she's right. It's just that I wish I had one, to remind me to pray to Our Lady as well.'

A week later a gold medal and chain arrived

for Ursula, 'with lots of love from Uncle Frank and Aunty Iris'. She showed it to me and then put it away in her locker: she never wore it, of course.

6

We had been at the convent for almost a year, the routines and disciplines becoming familiar and habitual. As, physically, we became accustomed to a system where we were expected to control and regulate ourselves, the necessary mental adjustments were more difficult to achieve. The penalties for transgression were reiterated often. We were on our honour to accomplish the prescribed punishments without overt supervision, and the grievous hurts we were inflicting on God or Our Lady were impressed upon us over and over again.

Caro and I didn't talk about it much any more. To a watchful eye she accomplished everything that was expected of her, and once or twice when I asked her if she was all right she gave me the same answer as before, 'I'm all right, Bel. Don't ask me any more, just leave me alone.'

I knew that she wasn't all right, that the constant pressure to seek perfection in all that we did was harder for her than for me. I was used to falling short of what was expected of me, but until we went to the convent Caro had been indulged in a way that would never happen here.

She began to develop a personal armour against the intrusions of religion and the verbal invasions of our privacy which surrounded and assailed us daily. She became amusing. It wasn't a clever disguise, but from somewhere inside herself she found an ingenuous, charming persona, one which excluded me as surely as it kept the incursions of the nuns at bay, for I took a different path, one which led, eventually, to submission.

My life became a battleground for the avoidance of sin; of knowledge that even if I *did* something good, my thoughts might betray me, for sin committed in the heart was worse than sin actually committed. The more frightened I was the more I was grateful for the punishments, because for a while at least the terror in my heart was quiet.

Mother Benedict had told us that to put a stone in one's shoe was a good way to obtain submission of the flesh. I had a belt made of chain which went with a dress I wore on Saturdays and I wore this belt under my vest, done up so tightly that blisters appeared through every link. It hurt so terribly that I felt sure that I must have gained some remission from purgatoy, but when a horrified Caro saw the marks around my waist, she threatened to tell Mother Patrick and hid the belt. She was younger than me but understood better than I how to adapt in this alien territory.

Towards the end of that first year we became aware of some excitement in the air and gossip from day girls confirmed that something unusual was happening. The day girls were carefully cultivated as the only source of secrecy in the convent. All our letters, except those to our parents, had to be left unsealed and when a letter was received with unknown handwriting on the envelope, Mother Bernard had to read it and it was then put out with the envelope slit open. Everyone hated the system and sometimes one of the older girls would be told that an unsuitable letter was being forwarded to her parents. The day girls could demand practically anything in payment for smuggling letters in and out.

They had heard talk about the convent moving and one evening after supper Reverend Mother herself came into the refectory. She had a very characteristic way of walking, leaning forward slightly, which always gave her movements an air of urgency rather unusual in a nun. She clapped her hands for silence.

'I have a wonderful surprise for you. Tomorrow we are going on a picnic.' There were cheers for the summer outing was always fun, but Reverend Mother went on, 'No, it's not the outing but something more exciting than that. We are, as you must all be aware, very cramped here in this little convent and the Community has for a long time wanted to expand and to be able to have your playing fields near the school, and a swimming pool, and generally to have more room for everyone. I am happy to tell you, *very* happy to tell you, that we have managed to buy a much bigger house a few miles outside the town and that from next term all those of you over the age of twelve will be moving to the new school. Tomorrow all of you and the whole Community will be going to see our new home.'

The next day we drove for three miles up a gentle slope with green hills rolling away in all directions. Green, shadowy hollows lay where one hill gave way to another, the clouds making moving patterns on the rounded tops. Trees, still newly green, gathered together or stood singly in the fields and the haze of early summer softened everywhere we looked.

The coaches turned sharply off the road, between two stone gateposts standing empty and unfilled. For half a mile we drove past fields on either side of the drive, with the kind of ornamentally planted trees that make up parkland on an estate. Rusty iron fences corralled sheep, and rooks floated and quarrelled above them.

Suddenly, to our left was a great golden house, with a tiny golden chapel near by, a carpet of new green grass in front of it and dark cedar trees all around it. Wide, shallow steps led up to the front door, which stood open to welcome us. A parapet ran around the top storey of the house and wide windows with delicate wooden glazing bars flashed in the sunshine. This was a fairytale house and soon fifty of us would actually live here with gardens and woods stretching as far as we could see.

We climbed out of the coaches and Mother Patrick and Mother Benedict divided us into two groups.

'My group will start at the front of the house,'

said Mother Patrick, 'and Mother Benedict's group will start at the back. We shall all meet up for lunch and then,' she paused for dramatic effect, 'and then, we shall all go round the gardens. Oh! and they are such gardens. My group follow me, please.'

She led us up the low golden steps circling in a half-moon around the door. It was so hot outside and so cool in the house. A narrow outer hall had two doors, one at each end of it. The right-hand door opened into a cloakroom of buff marble and pink-tinted mirrors, like something in a Hollywood film and not like a convent at all. At the other end of the hall a door opened into what Mother Patrick was already describing as the Painted Parlour. It was a small circular room and the walls were covered from floor to ceiling with paintings of clouds and fat cherubim in soft pinks and blues. The ceiling was dark-blue and dotted with golden stars. We were all amazed into silence. I couldn't believe the nuns would leave naked babies on view like that, but they did and it became an incongruous sight to see Reverend Mother sitting upright and dignified amongst so much abandonment.

This little hall opened into a much larger inner hall, the light-well soaring to the very top of the house. The floor was of black wood and there were tall, panelled doors dotted around this inner space. Before we could look behind any of them we saw first, with mounting astonishment, a huge curving staircase with a handrail of ribbed, emerald-green glass, twisting up out of sight above our heads. In a dark corner under the turn of the stairs was a golden fretted door to a lift, shaped like an immense bird's cage. Mother Patrick called this the Parrot's Cage, and so it became for ever.

An archway and a passage led off to the right and we could hear Mother Benedict's voice coming from that direction, so we went towards the door on the other side of the wide black hall. The room we rushed into was huge and empty. A wide, carved fireplace and tall wooden shutters were the only things to break the monotony of the walls, and there were two sets of bow windows. One looked over a little sunken garden with a green, slimy-looking pond surrounded by statues and all wrapped round by a yew hedge; from the other we could see garden and park stretching away until they disappeared into the haze. I wondered if the big empty room had been a ballroom, it had such a romantic aspect.

In the far wall there was a doorway like a cupboard, and stepping out of it on the other side we were in a library, no doubt of that as empty bookshelves, painted a soft duck-egg blue, ran around the walls and up to the ceiling. There were french windows on to a terrace and another door through which we passed into a shadowy, echoing room from which led a long stone passage with doors leading off it on either side — the kitchens, gym, locker rooms, common rooms and drying-room, now all empty and echoing and unbelievable.

We leapt up another staircase, ran along a corridor, up more stairs and found ourselves looking down into the black hall, leaning over that astonishing emerald glass banister.

'This floor,' said Mother Patrick, 'is where the dormitories will be,' and she opened doors to show us big rooms full of light and all with views over fields and trees. There were four wonderful bathrooms. The best one was in a room as big as any of the bedrooms, where the walls and ceiling were covered entirely with mirror glass. The bath stood on a platform with the tap end against the wall and on either side of the bath, like two thrones, each in an alcove, were two lavatories. It was the most arresting sight we had so far seen.

This improbable room became the sacristy, where Father Ryan robed himself and prepared the wine and wafers for Holy Communion on a corner of the pink marble washstand, and where he heard our confessions. Next door to this bewitching bathroom was the chapel, a room already consecrated, as the house had belonged since it was first built, in the time of the Regency, to one of the old Catholic families of England.

Three more bathrooms were sequentially revealed, each had a huge, deep bath and an elaborate shower enclosed in a cage of pipes. I saw with relief that all the bedrooms had hot and cold taps in the washbasins.

It was difficult to take it all in at once but there was a cloud hovering over me all the time. Caro wouldn't be twelve until next year and Reverend

Mother had said that only those of us over twelve were going to move into this Box of Delights. I hated the thought of Caro staying in the grey garden of the convent in town, breaking the ice on her water jug in the winter and enduring the burning, itching chilblains which were as regular as winter itself. I wondered what I could do.

We hadn't yet seen the chapel but Mother Patrick told us that we would have that pleasure before we went home. Instead, she took us away from the bedrooms, down an outside staircase to an enclosed cobbled yard. There was a row of low buildings, like the middle stroke of an E, which formed one side of the yard and this was to be the Chaplain's house. The top of the E would be where the Community lived, out of bounds and shielded by high shrubs and a bank from the rest of the gardens. A large rockery with steps helped further to isolate the nuns from the rest of the school. From the cobbled yard, down steps to the real backyard, through an archway, and we were back at the front of the house.

We were excited and unusually noisy but I noticed as the tour of the house progressed that Mother Patrick was much less energetic than I would have expected. She had started the day in as high spirits as any of us, as she had already seen the house and was delighting in our joy and freedom, but now, as we jumped down the steps to the lower yard, she stopped half-way down and seemed to be having difficulty in breathing, leaning against the pitted metal handrail fitted to the wall.

For some reason I noticed with great clarity small green fronds of fern and the tiny purple flowers of toadflax growing out of cracks in the brickwork and I remembered that in Cornwall we had called the toadflax mother of thousands.

Oona McKenna, who was one of the older girls in our group and a sister of my friend Carmel, stopped by Mother Patrick to see if she was all right. I didn't hear what Mother Patrick said to her but as soon as Oona had turned out of Mother Patrick's sight under the archway, she ran to Reverend Mother who was waiting with Mother Benedict and her group for us to catch up with them. Oona spoke to Reverend Mother, who said something quietly to Mother Benedict and then picked up the hem of her skirt so that she wouldn't be slowed down and hurried into the backyard with Oona.

Mother Benedict seemed very much at home in this house and garden and happier than I had ever seen her. She called us together.

'After all this excitement I expect you are ready for something to eat. If you go round to the terrace at the back of the house you will find that Sister Bridget and Sister Gabriel have put your picnic lunches out for you. You may eat them in the garden but please don't wander too far away as we have a lot more to see after lunch.'

I tried to move back towards the archway into the yard to see if Mother Patrick was there but Mother Benedict called for me to go with the others before moving off in that direction herself.

Wicker laundry baskets full of packets of sandwiches and small apple pies were waiting for us on the terrace, where a picnic table had been set up to hold jugs of home-made lemonade. There didn't seem to be anyone to supervise us so we split into groups and I sat with Antonia and Patsy. Flowers spilled in abandon all over the stones; little yellow buttercups bursting into the patches of blue gentians, pansies spreading into the primulas and already the pink stalks of the sempervivum flowers rose like candlesticks out of bitter-green rosettes. Dry, crunchy mounds of yellow alyssum, dying down but still host to hovering bees, edged the steps. In front of us a neglected lawn was starred with buttercups and daisies and the long rough branches of a huge cedar tree spread shade over the grass. A patch of rhododendron bushes topped a bank which sloped gently away to our right, with a gravel path curving around it. I could smell the most overpoweringly sweet scent.

'Wonder what happened to Paddy — did anyone see?'

'I saw her on the steps and Oona fetched Reverend Mother so I expect she's OK. Too much excitement, I should think. And no wonder, have you ever seen anything like that bathroom?'

'They'll never let us use it with all those mirrors, might lead to sin, seeing our girlish bodies all over the place like that.'

'I expect they'll paint over the naked babies too, but wasn't it super. That dear little lift and all the space in the world.'

Mary Clare, who had been sitting near us, suddenly got up and ran towards the cedar tree and was half-way up the main trunk by the time Mother Benedict, appearing from nowhere, had crossed the grass.

'Get down at once, Mary Clare.' Mary Clare dropped neatly on her feet by the nun. 'I will not have such an immodest exhibition of legs from such a big girl. Do you *quite* understand that, Mary Clare Duffy?'

Mary Clare, who came from a long line of immodest showers of legs, managed to appear unconcerned at the same time as conveying to Mother Benedict that she was contrite. It was a well-honed skill of hers. She decided on a distraction.

'Is Mother Patrick all right, Mother?' she asked. 'We were all just wondering about her.'

'Mother Patrick is quite well again, thank you, it was just a touch of indigestion and when she's had a rest, she'll be ready for a walk around the grounds. No more climbing, girls, and put your rubbish in the baskets, *not* in the flower beds, Patsy Meredith.'

She started to walk in the direction of the house but turned back to face us.

'Has anyone seen Ursula Hosier since you started your lunch?'

'No, Mother.' This was from all of us.

'Or Sister Gabriel?'

'Not since she put the lemonade out, Mother.'

'Thank you.' This time she did leave, golden pollen from the buttercups marking her black skirt as she made her heavy-footed way into the house by the french windows.

'Wonder what the lovely Ursula is up to with Sister Gabriel,' said Patsy, more interested in coaxing a string of ants to march across her apple pie than in where my cousin really was.

'How do you know they're together, Pats?' said Antonia, 'Benny probably just needs Ursula to run a message and she treats Sister Gabriel like a slave so she probably wants her to wash up or something.'

'Oh come *on*, Antonia,' this came from Regina, who had walked over to join us on the rockery. 'If Ursula's not getting what she calls "extra instruction" from Father Ryan, she's sure to be with Sister Gabriel, they're always together these days, even you must have noticed. No wonder the nuns are worried,' she went on, 'Ursula's a time-bomb waiting to explode and if we aren't careful we'll all go bang with her.'

She sounded tired, not like a girl at all and I wondered, as I often had, why Regina seemed so much older than the rest of us. She saw me looking at her and went on, 'Ask Isobel if you don't believe me. She knows what Ursula's like.'

And I did, of course. I knew how she so easily confused other people's notions of right and wrong; how everyone she met felt that Ursula had singled them out for their special qualities, and glowed and strutted to catch her eye and please her. I saw too how none of it meant anything to her. She was much too clever to hurt anyone's feelings, of course, and managed, like a puppeteer, to hold many strings in her hands at once, knowing which one to tighten and which to allow to become slack. Everyone hoped that she liked them but I knew that she liked no one, not even herself. I suspected that what Regina had said was true and I was apprehensive.

A whole posse of nuns came round the corner of the house; they were laughing and chattering together in a way I'd never seen before. They gathered up the empty laundry baskets and jugs and put everything inside the library and all of them, mothers and sisters, started to walk away from the house, down the gravelled path, fanning across the lawns. Mother Benedict and Mother Bernard gestured to all of us to accompany them.

I think it was this first sight of the nuns as a Community that made me really think about their lives and why they behaved towards us as they did. They were like happy children, enjoying themselves as unselfconsciously as any close family.

We came to what might once have been a gateway in a brick wall but was now just ivy-covered heaps of rubble. Ahead stretched a herbaceous border, neglected but lovely still in its cottage garden profligacy. Lupins and delphiniums rioted among iris and feathery astilbe; forget-me-nots and heart's-ease had seeded themselves in every empty patch of earth, and tangled in the overgrown grass were the heart-shaped leaves of alchemilla.

At the end of the border there was a statue;

a huge head that reminded me of Neptune in the gardens on Tresco. It wore a lopsided wig of crusty orange lichen. The path divided around it, before plunging into a grassy ride, dark except for the white lanterns of syringa which hung on every bush. This was the source of the sweet, strong smell which hung over the garden. In spite of the heat of the day it still felt damp in there but, like being in a railway tunnel, we could see sunlight at the end of it.

At some point, and afterwards I could never remember just when, I noticed Sister Gabriel helping Sister Bridget to pick posies of flowers from the overgrown borders to take back to decorate the statue in the corridor of the convent. I became aware too of Ursula walking near by. Wherever they had been, they were back now, and Ursula came over to me.

'Did Mother Benedict ask where I was, Bel?'

'Why do you want to know?' I couldn't be bothered with Ursula today.

'Because I wasn't feeling very well after the drive in the coach and I went to sit quietly on my own but Regina said that Benny was on the warpath as she couldn't find me.'

'Well, if Regina said that, I expect it's right, she doesn't tell lies. You'd better go and tell Mother Benedict that you're feeling better, no doubt she's worrying about her little pet.'

Ursula didn't look sick to me; with her flushed cheeks and her hair untidy she looked even prettier than usual. She grabbed my arm.

'Please, Isobel, if Benny asks, say that I wasn't well. Tell her that I'm always car sick, will you?'

'Tell her yourself,' I snapped and hurried to catch up with Stella, knowing that Ursula herself would be able to make a very convincing job of persuading Mother Benedict. I should have been more careful of course.

As we walked along the sun-speckled path Mother Benedict moved up behind me and said, 'Isobel!'

I turned towards her. 'Yes, Mother.'

'What is this I hear about you being glad that your sister is not able to move to the new school with you?'

'But Mother, of course I want Caro to come with us. It's stupid to say that I don't.'

'Don't be insolent, Isobel. I know it's the kind of thing you *would* say. Just what I would expect from you.'

I was stunned by the unfairness of this judgement; whatever marred my character, disloyalty to my sister was not part of it, and I burned with resentment that anyone should think so. Then, of course, I saw Ursula standing behind the big nun and saw the half-smile on Ursula's face, and knew the answer. She might be able to conceal her lies from Mother Benedict but not from me. Not now, not ever.

I tried to say that what Mother Benedict had heard just wasn't true, in the panicky, hopeless way of a child against an adult, but Ursula had done her job well and I retreated, hurt, and impotent to recover my good name. To my surprise, Mother Patrick, who had been listening quietly as we all walked together on the unmown grass, suggested that Ursula had misunderstood what I had said.

'There is a special dispensation for sisters, and Caroline will be coming to the new convent with Isobel,' she said, and as I walked on I heard her add to Mother Benedict, 'I'm surprised you should listen to Ursula Hosier's troublemaking. That girl needs watching, and where was she, may I ask? *Not* car sick, of that I'm sure.'

Mother Patrick was still awfully pale and was quiet and walking much more slowly than usual. She said that she felt quite all right but as soon as we reached the belvedere she went to sit on one of the white-painted seats which were protected by carved and fretted canopies of wood and which formed twin arcs, like open arms, on either side of the paved circular area, where the dark, sweet-smelling tunnel of trees had ended.

There was a waist-high parapet at the further side of the circle, where the land fell away to sweep in curves of yellow and green hills and valleys to the horizon. Horses grazed in buttercup fields, cows in the water meadows beside an ox-bowed silver river glittering in the sun. Smoke from a train, silently steaming between the hills and lazy little stations, hung in the hot, blue air of the Vale.

There were no flowers here in the belvedere to distract the eye from the view, other than tiny weeds pushing up through cracks between the golden flagstones. We sat for a while surreptitiously trying to sunbathe while the nuns grouped and regrouped, talking together softly.

I was walking past the seat where Mother Patrick, as white as the paint, sat with her hands clasped tightly together in her lap. Suddenly one of those bony hands shot out and caught my skirt.

'Come and sit here, Isobel, I want to talk to you.'

Reluctantly I sat on the edge of the seat next to her, wondering what I'd done wrong this time. In the shade, in the quiet under the peeling wooden canopy, I could hear her breathing; it sounded like dry leaves rustling in her throat. I looked at her and saw that her blue eyes, usually so bright and penetrating, were full of tears. I was as shocked as if she had torn off her veil and sat there with her shaven head exposed.

'Isobel, my dear child,' she stopped and I could hear the leaves rustling, 'things aren't always as you perceive them, you know. Nuns are people just like everyone else, with all the faults and hopes and emotions that everyone has. Sometimes, you see, we have too much emotion, too much passion in our hearts and that's why we enter the convent, to channel all that energy into good. Sometimes we never manage it but we *do* try — we spend our lives trying. Do you understand at all what I am saying?'

She had taken a man's handkerchief from her deep pocket and was wiping her eyes, holding in her other hand the little steel-rimmed glasses that cut so sorely into the bridge of her nose.

'I'm not sure, Mother Patrick. Do you mean about Mother Benedict believing what Ursula said?'

'Mother Benedict is a good nun, Isobel, and sometimes she finds it very hard to accept that not everyone is as good as she is.'

She seemed so small and tired suddenly and I wasn't afraid of her at all. I wondered if she had finished talking to me, but she put her handkerchief away and went on, 'There is something I am trying to explain to you, child, and you must try and understand.'

From the corner of my eye I could see Regina and Mary Clare wriggling their skirts above their knees, long white legs and short, curvy brown ones stretched out in the sunshine.

'You may think that we are sometimes unfair, that we expect a higher standard from you than from some of the other girls. We expect you to go to Mass *every* morning and where others are only reprimanded for laziness or being less than truthful, you are punished. We put you on your honour a great deal of the time too, don't we? I know it's hard, Isobel, but you should be glad.'

She seemed to be having such difficulty in breathing that I was frightened to look at her and just nodded my head, trying not to see her blue lips.

'We only expect a lot from those whom we know are capable of giving it. Try to accept what you regard as unfairness as a test from God. Learn to say "Fiat" as Our Lady did and accept whatever God wants of you.'

She paused and her breath rattled in her throat. She closed her eyes and I slid off the seat but before Mother Bernard could take my space next to her, Mother Patrick sat up and, looking straight into my eyes, said very clearly to me, 'There are those in the Community who *know*, Isobel. You are not alone, child, always remember that.'

I needed to be on my own now though, to try and understand what the usually fearsome little nun had been trying to tell me, so I started to walk slowly back in the direction of the house. Before I got to Neptune's head I heard running footsteps behind me and Oona rushed past, shouting, 'Get out of the way, Isobel. Paddy's collapsed and I've got to run to the farm to phone for the ambulance.'

7

Mother Patrick died three days later. Three days when we, unbidden, walked and played quietly, and willingly offered up our indulgences, saved like holy Green Shield stamps, to allow Mother Patrick some remission from purgatory.

The open coffin was placed in a small changing room next to the gym, the smell of flowers and beeswax candles masking its usual musty, plimsoll odour. I didn't want to see her; I didn't need proof that she was dead, but we were all lined up in a silent crocodile to walk past the coffin.

Mother Patrick was dressed in her habit and on her head was a chaplet of white roses — the one she had worn for her Profession and saved for over forty years for her to wear when she was buried. My heart was thumping as I took the branch of boxwood and made the sign of the cross, drops of holy water spattering on her hands. She didn't look much like Mother Patrick at all, now the bold, blue eyes were closed by papery-white eyelids. She was so small, dead, that I thought she looked like a child ready to go to a fancy dress party and I wondered how I could ever have been so frightened of her. Someone had twined her rosary into her bony hands and the only other things that she possessed, her Office and the steel-rimmed glasses, were on the table by her feet, next to the glass bowl of holy water.

I had enjoyed a brief flicker of notoriety as the last person Mother Patrick had spoken to before she had slipped quietly into the unconsciousness from which she never woke. I had been puzzled by what she had said to me and now I felt a frightening obligation to understand, as if I had been handed the distillation of her forty years of experience, of self-denial and discipline. I *did* understand that she knew about Ursula and that, somehow, she knew that behind my outward reluctance was a tiny flame waiting only for the right spark to ignite it, to scorch and cauterise. I was too young to carry the torch she had handed to me and too frightened of the immediacy of death to want to entertain her in my mind.

We knew, of course, that some of the nuns were visited from time to time by their families; we saw them walking in the garden and once or twice guiltily loitered in the corridor to eavesdrop on crying and a raised voice coming from the parlour. Mother Clare was even quieter than usual after one of these episodes, but it was difficult to reconcile the two heavy middle-aged men buttoned tightly into bright-brown suits with Mother Patrick. There were one or two younger men and women, all with the same rusty hair, and three women whose reluctant corseting creaked every time they genuflected.

I had time to notice all this as I had been chosen, with Stella, to lead the funeral procession: Oona and Deirdre Byrne as Head Girls were bringing up the rear. The Community didn't come with us, of course, and although I tried to think about Mother Patrick and offer up prayers for the repose of her soul, all I could concentrate on was the grotesque, hunchbacked figure of the undertaker's assistant, who sat crouched and leering in the back of the hearse, two yards in front of us as we walked through the town, from the convent to the cemetery.

He had a face like polished brass, his nostrils seeming to flare over his cheeks, and his determination to make us laugh was as dogged as he was disquieting. I didn't like to think of Mother Patrick sharing her last ride with this gargoyle so tried to imagine how her eyes would have creased in merriment and her mouth tightened to avoid a laugh escaping at this indelicate juxtaposition.

A convent is like a machine and when a part breaks down, a replacement is drawn from the stores and the machine moves forward with scarcely a break in its rhythm.

Reverend Mother told us that Mother Michael, who was Deputy Head in one of our sister houses, was to replace Mother Patrick as our Headmistress when we moved to the new school. In the meantime we were to regard Mother Clare as being in charge of us until the end of term. It was only because we liked Mother Clare and didn't want her to be in trouble that she managed to exert any control over us at all.

Perhaps she was lucky, too, that the annual Retreat was due and enforced silence descended like stifling fog over the whole convent. Apart from lessons — and we were enjoined not to speak more than necessary even then — we had to keep silence from after Benediction on Sunday evening until after Mass on the following Saturday. We were allowed one hour's recreation every day but no letters were distributed to bring us a reminder of the outside world and our only reading was religious books, specially set aside for the Retreat. We were supposed to stay away from our usual companions, reading and practising contemplation on our own. Every day there was a talk given by the visiting Retreat Master and we were encouraged to go to these and to ask to speak to him individually if we had a personal problem. The nuns took it in turns to read to us during those silent meals and we had to ask for water or bread by gesture instead of words. It was too long and too hard a discipline for children and those who broke the silence were not punished. I was surprised at this.

Antonia's birthday fell right in the middle of the Retreat and the day passed unmarked, except for a telephone call from her grandmother, which she was allowed to take in Mother Benedict's office.

Some of the older girls had met Mother Michael and told us gleefully how lucky they were to be leaving school so that they wouldn't have to have her as their Headmistress.

'Everyone at Regina Caeli is terrified of her,' Oona told us, 'she's an absolute demon about truthfulness and obedience. They say she's like the Gestapo and questions and questions you until you'll confess to anything. And she hasn't got any sense of humour, not like poor old Paddy. You could always make her laugh if you knew how.'

I missed Mother Patrick and knew that my sinfulness had hastened her death. If I hadn't argued all the time about what Caro and I were being taught to believe; if I had cheerfully accepted the punishments she had given me to help me curb my troublesome nature, perhaps she would still be alive.

One day, a few weeks after Mother Patrick's death, I was sitting in detention, grey uneven stitches being unpicked over and over again from my needlework, the intention being to teach me to control my hasty temper, when Mother Clare unexpectedly asked me what was really troubling me. I tried to explain that I had helped to kill Mother Patrick and to my astonishment Mother Clare laughed and said that if that was the case, then I should be very pleased with myself.

'It was nothing to do with you, Isobel. We all knew that Mother Patrick had a weak heart and all that's happened is that she has got to heaven before the rest of us and we are all glad and happy for her. That's why you never see any of us miserable about a death — we know that it's only the gateway through which we have to pass to start the best part of our life. Mother Patrick longed for the day she could join Our Lord in heaven, and now she has.'

She looked at me. 'Does that make you feel any better?'

'Yes, Mother,' I said. What else could I say?

'We're going to have a struggle to make a needlewoman out of you, Isobel. I'll finish that,' and kind Mother Clare took out of my hands the crumpled little altar cloth I had been attempting to hem. Her own hands were soft and plump and she had shiny pink nails like little Venus shells. Her face often looked sad and she would press her lips together as if she were imprisoning words that would fly from them unchecked if she didn't take care.

All we saw of the nuns were their faces and their hands and sometimes a forearm, wrinkly or freckled, if a sleeve slipped back unchecked. Even in the height of summer they wore thick black stockings and when they lifted the skirt of their habit to tuck it into the wide leather belt worn around their waist, which they did to keep it clean, there was another equally heavy black underskirt between them and our gaze.

I had seen their underwear drying in the boiler room on an expedition out of bounds; vests, darned on darns until scarcely any of the original fabric showed and strips of cloth like wide, hemmed bandages. It was Regina who told me that these were used to bind down their breasts and I wondered how she knew such a strange thing.

The habit was impenetrable but everything about Mother Clare was soft and round and quiet and she was kind even to the undeserving — perhaps especially to them.

'Go and get some fresh air now, Isobel.'

I closed my sewing box thankfully and went towards the door but Mother Clare spoke again.

'Isobel, Mother Patrick thought highly of you, you know. Perhaps I shouldn't tell you so but I don't want any more of this nonsense about killing her. It's an indulgence for you to think like that and you must resist it. Go on now.' She was already finishing my hated needlework as I escaped.

The term drew to its close. Caro and I packed the big trunk, excited at the thought of eight weeks away from rules and discipline. What pleased me most was the knowledge that Ursula was flying out to join her mother in San Francisco and I would be free of her for the first time in a year.

Caro and I knew that we were going to Cornwall and I could only let the thought seep into my mind in small trickles as my heart thumped so with excitement. The barley would be ready to cut and blackberries ready to pick before we had to come back to London. The ponies would be there to ride in gymkhanas and the sea. Oh! the sea was always there, waiting for us.

We left the little grey convent and journeyed home together to the clammy suburb where we lived. We were two separate beings now in a way we hadn't been a year ago, but I knew that my sister was just as excited as I was. Cornwall was home, wherever we had to live. Our grandparents would be waiting for us and we would sleep in the room that had been our father's, gulls flying around the roof and the smell of seaweed on the wind.

8

We travelled alone on the train from Paddington, hot and fidgety, every seat in the carriage taken and the corridor full of people and luggage. When we reached Penzance we peered through the steam rising high into the glass roof of the station, to see who had come to meet us, and there was our grandfather waving his stick in greeting as if it were a sword. We ran along the platform as fast as we could, our suitcases banging against our legs.

'Straight home, Hockin. Take the road by the sea,' and we settled into the back of the big old car, one on each side of him.

The bird's eggs were still in their glass cases on the wall above the chest of drawers; the Rugby caps on their hooks, gold silk tassels hanging in a fringe over the bookcase. Our books, mine and Caro's, were on the shelves and night-lights stood in saucers of water on the bedside tables ready for my grandmother to light when she kissed us goodnight.

When I woke that first morning the sun was just rising above the horizon and I pulled down the brown holland blind and let it rattle upwards, the little wooden acorn at the end of the string pinging against the glass. Caro stirred and muttered but burrowed into the blankets. Her bed looked as if it had been the site of some nocturnal battle. It always did and I could never understand how someone who slept as if she had died could make such a mess of the bedclothes.

The bedroom was at the side of the house and I could see over the hydrangeas and fuchsia bushes to the wall which divided the lower garden from the house of Miss Clarrie and Miss Avril Lemon who lived next door to my grandparents. There were espaliered pear trees along the wall and in the front of the beds were perfect, tiny pink roses grown especially for my grandmother.

There was still dew on the shaggy grass next door and an indigo shadow thrown by the dividing wall. Sometimes Miss Avril came out wearing her father's old coat to walk barefoot in the grass, drinking from a big blue cup and smoking one cigarette after another. I waited, listening to the birds and watching the shadows changing shape, hoping she would appear.

I couldn't see the back door but a lozenge of light appeared on the gravel path and I imagined the sound of Miss Avril's cough in the cool morning air. She came around the corner of the house wearing a man's dress shirt and enormous jodhpurs pulled tightly into her waist by a striped tie. Her hair was white, except for the fringe which was nicotine-yellow, and tied back into a ponytail. She looked about seventeen, the same age as the boy trailing through the grass with her. They were like ghost walkers, blurred by the shadows of the trees and I longed to be with them, another ghost in the empty, dewy garden.

'There's a boy next door,' I said to my grandmother at breakfast, 'I saw him with Miss Avril.'

'That's Jack Frost,' she said. I looked at her to see if she meant it. I had never known my grandmother not to have an answer to a question, the trick was to ask her something twice to see if you got the same answer both times. It worked well when she was showing someone around the garden.

'Oh that, I believe it's Proboscis Purpurea. Unusual, don't you think?' and she would move on to firmer ground.

She continued to cut her breakfast apple into little slivers with her special knife.

'He is called Jack Frost and just for the moment he's staying with Clarrie and Avril.'

My grandfather snorted behind the *Western Morning News.*

'I thought Emerald had more sense than to leave the boy with those two old hens. Wouldn't trust them with a dog of mine.' He folded the paper and stood up.

'Back on the treadmill, I suppose. Anyone want to come to the abattoir with me this morning?'

My grandmother gave a hoot of laughter. She was a very small woman who looked as fragile and delicate as her special pink roses, but she had a laugh I'd heard my grandfather describe as being like something heard in a four-ale bar on a Saturday night.

'Don't be ridiculous, Archie. Of course no one wants to go near that beastly place.'

'Oh well, another day then.' He dropped a kiss on the top of Caro's head, then mine, and two new half-crowns appeared by our plates.

'Wages. For looking after your grandmother while I'm out. Shan't be in to lunch, May, got some business to see to.'

He went regularly to see the animals being slaughtered and had been asking me to go to the abattoir with him for as long as I could remember but I couldn't remember how the joke had started.

He went stamping out of the dining-room and there was a silence like the absence of noise left behind after a great wind. My grandmother finished her apple and then rang the bell for Sonja Hockin to come and clear away the breakfast things.

Sonja, the daughter of my grandfather's driver, was new since we had last stayed with our grandparents. Her mother had been entranced by Sonja Henie's skating but if she had hoped the name might influence her unborn daughter's appearance, she was to be disappointed, for Sonja Hockin had heavy arms and legs that seemed almost too wide to join comfortably to her body, her waist was small and her chest completely flat. In place of the bouncing blonde curls her name would suggest was a bob of shiny, almost black hair and her small brown eyes darted with intelligence. She had a faint but noticeable moustache.

As she cleared away cutlery and crusts she was watching us sideways, just as we were evaluating her. Her arms were speckled with freckles like the brown eggshells she piled on to her tray. My grandmother had moved to rearranging roses in a silver bowl on a table under the window.

'Well, my dears, have you a plan for today? I shall be busy in the garden, of course, but you must do just whatever you like. Lunch is at one o'clock. Just three today, Sonja,' she said, turning to the girl, 'and visitors at tea time. Perhaps one of your wonderful lemon curd sponges?'

She continued to tantalise the flowers and went on, 'Jack Frost is coming to tea so that he can meet you and I've asked his aunts as well as I know they are great favourites of yours, Isobel.'

'Oh, wizard,' I said, 'they're so interesting, is he like them, Gran?'

'I rather think he *is* like them, yes.'

There was a sound like a choked-off cough from Sonja's departing back and my grandmother sighed.

'Such a good cook but not quite —' she paused, 'not quite — oh well. I've dead-heading to do,' she continued more briskly, 'see you at lunch time, dears.'

My grandmother gathered up the bunch of keys which hung on a fine silver chain from her belt, one of which opened the store room where tins and bottles and lavatory paper and candles — and every other necessity for the running of the household — were kept, and went to find a jar of lemon curd for Sonja.

Left to ourselves Caro and I didn't have to wonder what we were going to do. Our swimming things were already rolled inside their towels on our beds and we ran up the wide, red-carpeted stairs to fetch them. We crashed out of the side door, making the little blue and yellow glass panes shudder. We didn't care, we were free and going to the beach.

After lunch our grandmother wrote letters. She wrote letters every day and this, together with the garden, was the circumference of her life, our grandfather only denting the edges a little. She had followed him from posting to posting, bearing children in heat and discomfort, only to lose them to boarding-school when they were still too young. Now she bullied the gardeners and dead-headed her flowers with an impressive ferocity.

She had put her letters on a small silver tray in the hall and was sitting with us in the morning-room, looking at *Picture Post*, squinting through the smoke from her Craven A. Caro and I were trying to find the pictures of First World War casualties in our grandfather's heavy, leather-bound books. I particularly liked the soldiers on crutches waving a cigarette cheerily at the camera but Caro preferred the columns of men with their eyes covered, walking like the ebony elephants on our grandfather's desk, each with a hand on the shoulder of the man in front. Caro was learning how to whistle and every now and then a reedy piffle would escape into the silence.

We heard Sonja scuffing along the tiled floor of the hall. She was wearing a pair of our grandmother's old shoes and as they were too small for her she had broken the backs down and wore them like jaunty Turkish slippers. She had perfected a curious shuffle to keep them on her feet at all. We hadn't noticed the front door bell but heard Sonja say, 'Good afternoon, Miss Lemon, Miss Avril.'

She opened the door of the morning-room and a mesmerising little cavalcade came in. For several years Clarrie Lemon had modelled herself on Queen Mary and today she wore mauve. A small toque covered in violets, a choker of pearls and even, oh glory, a parasol. Her shoes, which just showed under the hem of her lace gown, were of pale-mauve satin, very worn and muddy.

Avril Lemon still wore the jodhpurs and shirt I had first seen her in that morning but had formalised the effect by adding a number of strings of beads and she was carrying an enormous crocodile handbag.

Following his aunts through the doorway was Jack Frost. He wasn't very tall and he never did grow quite tall enough. I learned to understand that it was something that irked him but he would never admit it, standing very straight to conceal his lack of height. He had a wide mouth with strong teeth and his nose was too big for his face but it was his eyes that I saw so often afterwards in my imagination. That day they were grey, like the sea in winter, but sometimes, wearing his blue Aertex shirt, they were the colour of a summer sky. Sometimes they looked almost navy-blue like the shadows on the morning grass. It was a most uncommon thing.

Why, in that moment of introduction, did an image of Ursula pass over my mind like a hand shielding my eyes from the light? Ursula couldn't hurt me here but perhaps she had come to embody everything I was afraid of and I already knew that I wanted to keep Jack separate and unscathed.

He was saying something to me.

'Sorry,' I muttered, 'sorry, I was miles away.'

'I said I saw you this morning. At the window, when Aunt Avril and I went looking for the tortoise. It's a very dull sort of animal but Avril loves it.'

'Oh!' I was confused as I had thought my morning observation unobserved and could think of nothing to say. 'Did you find it?'

'No. Probably in your grandfather's lettuces again. If you see it, push it back through the hedge, will you? He said if he found it in his garden again, he'd kill it.'

'He might do that, you know, he seems to like dead animals. Perhaps it reminds him of being in the army.'

Jack laughed, he understood my joke.

Sonja wheeled in the tea trolley and placed it beside my grandmother's chair. There were sandwiches with the crust cut off, a bowl of tiny, shiny tomatoes which my grandmother ate with her tea every day, scones and a cut-glass dish of thick, crusty cream, seedy cake and the lemon curd sponge. The cups were old and fragile, pink roses and dark-green leaves circling the edges of the plates, and small silver teaspoons shining in the saucers.

Clarrie Lemon was giving a passable imitation of Queen Mary, very gracious and cordial. She had a willing audience in Caro, who seemed captivated by the faded violets and stained satin shoes, her eyes darting from one to the other as she tried to hold Clarrie's interest by telling her about the pictures of the casualties we had just been looking at. Avril left the room twice, carrying the crocodile handbag with her. It wasn't something that one noticed, of course.

I tried not to look at Jack as I knew that everyone in the room would surely notice each time that I did and I had learned even then that it was safer to keep one's feelings hidden. As he stretched out his hand across a beam of sunlight the hairs on his wrist and forearm looked like soft gold wire and I felt a knot in my throat, so odd that I could hardly swallow.

When they had gone and Caro and I were sitting in the kitchen watching Sonja wash up, she asked if we'd had a nice tea party.

'And what did you think of Master Jack then? Reckon you'll get on all right, do you?'

This was dangerous ground so I said he was OK and quickly asked Sonja why Miss Clarrie had worn such funny clothes.

'Well, my dad says she's never been right since her young man was killed in the First War. You didn't ought to go on about they old pictures, Miss Caro, but I suppose you didn't know.'

Caro said, 'I thought her clothes were lovely; I shall dress like that when I'm old enough. Tell us about her young man, Sonja.'

Sonja turned around and leaned against the old stone sink while she wiped her hands on her apron.

'Your grandmother don't like me to gossip.'

'Please, please Sonja. We won't tell *anyone* that you gossip, will we, Bel?'

Sonja loved an audience so she folded her freckly arms and started.

'Well, he was the middle son of the Bonallacks over to Treave and was supposed to be the best-looking of all they boys and they'm some handsome family, as you do know. He and Miss Clarrie were born on the same day and they'd been meant for each other ever since they were babies and everyone knew they'd get married. Mind you, she was a catch too. Have you seen the picture of her in the drawing-room next door?'

'The one where she's wearing a white dress and has feathers in her hair?'

' 'Es that's the one. She was eighteen when that was painted and my dad said she was the prettiest girl he ever saw. Her and Edgar Bonallack got engaged but every time they wanted to set a date to get married her old dad kept thinking up reasons why she had to wait a bit longer. First he said she was too young and then she had to run the house as her stepmother wasn't strong enough to do it. The only thing wrong with *her* was that she was too lazy to get out of her own shadow, idle toad.' Sonja paused for a moment, her face maliciously amused. 'Shall I tell you something about her?'

'Oh yes, please,' we spoke together, this was exciting.

'All right, but don't you let on then, that I've told you. Well, she used to be Miss Clarrie's and Miss Avril's nursemaid you see and when their mother died, old man Lemon upped and married *her*. My dad don't remember it, of course, but he've heard the tale enough times and it was a proper scandal at the time my dad says. But that's another story.'

Sonja was enjoying herself now and went on, 'They were engaged for years and then of all things, the Great War started and Edgar Bonallack and his brothers went and joined the army, Duke of Cornwall's Light Infantry same as your grandfather. 'Twas a terrible thing but all three of they Bonallack boys was killed and when Miss Clarrie heard that her Edgar wasn't coming back she locked herself in her room and wouldn't come out. The only person she would speak to was Miss Avril and *she never spoke another word to her father as long as he lived.*'

'Oh Sonja, did she go mad overnight and never change her clothes and let the mice eat her food, like Miss Havisham?' Caro was enthralled.

'I don't know about no Miss Havisham, my bird,

and poor Miss Clarrie wasn't mad, not *really* mad, I suppose these days you'd say she had a nervous breakdown but my dad says she's never been too clever ever since.'

'Your dad knows an awful lot, Sonja,' said Caro.

'Oh 'es, 'e do knaw, as we say, 'e do knaw all right.'

She smiled a secret smile and I thought she had finished her story but after a little pause when she seemed to be far away, she went on.

'My dad has always worked for your grandfather, you know, and my grandad worked for your great-grandfather so there's not much we Hockins *don't* know.'

This time she *had* finished and turned to the black Cornish range for a kettle of hot water to finish washing up the tea things.

Whatever business our grandfather had been seeing to that day must have gone well and he was in a peaceful mood. We were eating crab salad, which was his favourite, and he was cracking the spidery legs and sucking juice and meat out of the shells with a terrible slurping noise. Caro looked at me with her eyes sparkling and I knew she was going to copy him. She began an elaborate charade of her own.

'Be quiet, Caroline,' he roared, 'I'm allowed to do it because I'm a disgusting old man but I don't want to have to listen to you.'

We giggled because we knew he *couldn't* hear her: the reason that he shouted so was because he was deaf. He picked at the claws with a little silver hook and then said to our grandmother,

'Saw The Girls leaving this afternoon. Noticed Avril had her handbag with her, what did she borrow this time?'

My grandmother laid her napkin on the table. Her voice was shaking as she said,

'The silver tray from the hall, the bell from the table in here and a spare light bulb from the lavatory.'

She began one of her hooting laughs and we all joined in although neither Caro nor I knew just what we were laughing at. We laughed until our grandmother had to wipe the tears from her eyes and our grandfather started to cough.

'Good old Avril,' he said, coughing and wheezing.

'I thought of sending Isobel to borrow them back after dinner. What do you think, Archie?'

'Might as well, she's got to learn about the seamy side of life some time.'

I looked at him in alarm but he gave me a huge wink.

'Jack'll have rounded them up by now, I expect. A light bulb, dammit!' He laughed again and went back to his crabs' claws.

After dinner Sonja fetched one of the flat flower baskets and my grandmother told me to go next door to the Lemons.

'Now, I want you to get this quite right, Isobel. Say, very politely, "I wonder if it would be convenient to return the things that Miss Avril borrowed this afternoon." '

I rehearsed this little speech and then set off with the basket. I wasn't sure which door to go to because I knew the Lemons had no one to answer the bell for them. As I crunched up the drive I could smell the nicotianas planted under the windows. They were an odd, greeny colour which stood out in the half-light and as I hesitated, the front door opened and Jack stood in a pool of light in the front porch.

Before I had time to say the rehearsed words, he held out his hands, in which he held the magpie trove Miss Avril had removed that afternoon. I put them in the basket and he said, 'She can't help it, you know, and it *really is* only borrowing because everything is always returned, eventually. Most people know her and don't mind, but that awful man from London or somewhere, who's bought the shop where she buys her cigarettes, came round the other day and made the most awful fuss because she'd borrowed a pipe and some dummy packets of tobacco that he had on the counter.'

He leant against the door jamb and my heart started to thump. I wanted more than anything to stay here with him in the dusk with the smell of flowers around us, but I couldn't think of anything to say to delay my return with my booty.

Then Jack said, 'We could go swimming tomorrow if you like. Not in the morning as I've got to take the aunts to see the Bank Manager. They don't seem to have any money and there should be *some* at least. Would you like to?'

I couldn't remember ever feeling happier than I did just then and could only nod and crunch back down the drive with my basket of stolen silver.

9

Caro and I were both good swimmers but Jack swam like a seal, twisting and diving as if he belonged in the water. He had beautiful feet; square and strong, they looked as if they should have been carved in marble on a Roman statue.

We swam for a long time and then sat wrapped in towels to keep warm, eating saffron buns and drinking orange squash that Sonja had given us. Caro was sifting through piles of stones looking for little bits of broken glass. This part of the beach was always quiet because the visitors preferred to go further along where some sand was exposed when the tide went out and where there was less of an intimidating drop as the shingle shelved away steeply and unexpectedly under water. Suddenly Caro gave an excited squeak.

'Look what I've found.' She held up a rusty shilling. 'How lucky. I'll go and get us ice-creams.' She pulled a cardigan over her damp bathers and ran up the beach.

'Do you and your sister always go everywhere together?' Jack asked and I said that we did, that we liked it that way.

'Don't be cross,' he said, 'it's just that I thought

we could cycle to Marazion but we've only got two bikes.'

'Perhaps we could borrow another. I expect one of the Hockins could lend us one. I'll ask Sonja, if you like.'

Sonja said that the only bike they had that wasn't used every day belonged to her brother Eddy. It was much too small for him any more but Caro was smaller than Eddy and we were welcome to that if we wanted to try it.

I thought that Caro had got the best of it when Jack first wheeled his aunts' bicycles out of an empty greenhouse into the garden.

'They'll do us all right,' he said. Together we cleaned them and he patched the tyres, working with absolute concentration, his fingers deft and steady. Afterwards he scrubbed his hands clean and ran a small file under his nails. I was intrigued as I was used to our cousins' nails being broken and dirty and remembered that they only washed when they had to.

Caro practised cocking her leg over the crossbar of Eddy's bike and we set off for Marazion on a blue, windy day, with the reeds in the marsh teased by the wind into a landlocked imitation of the waves breaking not far away to our right.

We must have been an odd little procession, Jack leading the way with an ancient wicker picnic hamper strapped behind his saddle, Caro following him, wobbling about on Eddy Hockin's bike and me bringing up the rear on Clarrie Lemon's rusty, upright machine.

We stopped at Chyandour where the water always ran tinkling and clear under the little bridge on to the beach. Gulls were diving, shrieking hoarsely, in the wind which blew off the sea. We could see that the *Scillonian* was still anchored in the harbour and we laughed at the thought of the rough passage the visitors to the Islands were going to have that day, with the indifference of good sailors towards the seasick. Jack checked that the hamper was secure and we set off again. As we rode along we heard the Riviera Express behind us, catching up and passing us in clouds of steam on its daily journey to London.

With hindsight we all agreed we might have chosen a better day to try out our cycles. Soon we could hardly see the Mount through the mist, and the wind, which had been rising steadily, now funnelled through the narrow streets of Marazion, gusting and chilling.

We sat in a bus shelter, the rickety old bikes propped against the wall. It was the quiet time on a Saturday when the holidaymakers who were going home had left and the ones who were coming to take their place had not yet arrived. Beds were being changed, kitchens cleaned and the butcher and greengrocer had time to stop and gossip with their familiar customers. It was as if the whole of West Cornwall slackened and rested before putting on its welcoming smile again for another week.

'It's going to rain,' I said. Caro looked as if she was going to cry.

'I want to go home. I can't steer that horrible

bike and I'm cold.' She always looked colder than anyone else and her legs were mottled with blue patches like bruises. Jack suggested we ate our picnic and then went home.

'We'll be warmer on the beach if we wrap our towels around us and sit under the wall.'

There didn't seem to be anything better to do, so we pushed the bikes down the slipway and Jack unstrapped the hamper. Sonja had made us each a pasty early that morning and wrapped them in a tea towel so that they were still quite warm. Jack's was half as big again as mine and Caro's because Sonja thought, and she was probably right, that Jack didn't get enough to eat. There was a bottle of Corona, and ginger biscuits and three apples, but before we had finished eating a surge of wind blew sand and seaweed skittering up the beach to where we sat under the wall. Huge drops of rain began to fall, each one making its own little crater in the sand.

We threw everything into the basket and dragged the bikes back up the slipway before crouching again in the bus shelter, while it rained and rained, great slashing bursts of water like dripping curtains hanging between us and the rest of the world. As soon as it eased off a little, Caro jumped up. She wasn't weepy any more but very cross, standing in front of us like a small, angry bull.

'I don't care what you two do but I'm going home. And I'm never going to ride that hateful bike again. It was a horrible picnic and you're *both* horrible.'

We were so surprised, that she had swung her leg over the crossbar and wobbled a few yards down the road before either of us realised what she was doing. As she came to a bend in the road a lorry loaded with beer barrels overtook her and sent a bow wave of water washing over her. It was too much: she lost her precarious balance and fell, dragging Eddy's bike down on top of her.

It seemed that almost before I could understand what had happened, Jack was with Caro, lifting the bike off her and dragging her and the twisted machine out of the road. Caro's face was white and frightened and I could see puddles of blood, diluted by the rain, running down the gutter. Jack ran back to me.

'Go and ring your grandparents, Isobel. Tell them what's happened and that Caro's OK but her leg's badly cut. I know I shouldn't move her but I can't leave her lying in the road.'

He pulled some money out of his pocket and gave it to me without looking at it and then went back to my sister and I ran to the phone box on the corner. Through the smeary windows I could see him lifting Caro and staggering with her along the wet pavement as I tried, with shaking fingers, to push the pennies into the slot and speak coherently through chattering teeth.

I knew that it was my fault for not looking after Caro properly — I never had, just as my mother had always said — and now my sister was lying in a bus shelter with blood pouring out of a huge gash in her leg. I tried to remember all the prayers we had learned over the past year but didn't realise I was speaking aloud until Jack said sharply,

'Shut up, for goodness sake, Isobel. She's not dead, it's only a cut leg.'

I felt as if he had slapped me and as I looked across the road, trying not to cry, I saw a brown, wrinkled face looking out of a window straight at us. Two brown, wrinkled hands held back a net curtain but no one from the terrace of small houses ventured out into the rain, not a single person came to help us.

An ambulance arrived and I climbed in with Caro but Jack insisted on cycling home, wheeling my bike beside his. He tossed Eddy Hockin's buckled machine over the sea wall. Tom Jago, who ran a boat to and from the Mount found it later that evening when he was out looking for driftwood, and took it home for his youngest son.

Our grandmother was waiting at the hospital. She was perfectly calm and hugged and warmed me while Caro was out of sight having the dreadful cut in her leg stitched. I had stopped shivering and sobbing by the time Caro was wheeled out of the cubicle on a trolley. She looked pale and sleepy and I started to cry again.

'We're going to keep Caroline in hospital for tonight, Mrs Cuthbert, just to make sure everything's in order. She'll need to rest her leg for a while but she'll soon be as right as rain.' The young doctor stopped and said, 'That wasn't a very suitable analogy now, was it? Come on, young lady, if you keep crying like that we'll have to find a bed for you as well.'

I heard Caro saying sleepily, 'Where's Bel?' and I went and stood beside her.

'I'm sorry, Bel. It was my own fault, I shouldn't have gone off like that and I don't really think you're horrible.' She closed her eyes and was asleep, as quickly as a light being switched off.

From somewhere in the attics a wicker chaise-longue had been unearthed. It was thick with dust, its cushions fallen into shreds of faded green and red. Sonja had cleaned it and stood it outside the side door to air. My grandmother gave me a thick tartan rug for Caro to lie on and a cashmere shawl for her to snuggle into.

Hockin took our grandparents to fetch her home early the next morning and he carried her into the lower garden, where the chaise-longue was waiting in the sheltered corner where our grandparents often sat. Caro was still pale and quiet and seemed quite happy to settle down in her garden bed, the lovely old shawl around her shoulders and a pile of comics to read. I wanted to stay with her but I needed to go and find Jack.

I was still smarting from the way he had spoken so sharply to me and it was that, more than the accident, which had kept me awake so long the night before, tossing and turning, seeing in my mind's eye Caro's blood in the gutter. My grandfather had come into the bedroom with a small glass of brandy.

'No heel taps, Isobel. All in one go,' he said, and then, 'Good girl. Do you remember what I told you about eating an apple in the dark?'

I nodded. 'Never eat an apple in the dark because in the morning you may find half a maggot in the core.' I giggled and he kissed me goodnight. I did sleep then, but woke still aware that Jack despised me. I watched him and Miss Avril in the early, shadowy garden, talking as they walked together. I felt desolate, knowing I would never now be a part of that secret union.

I sat with Caro all morning, playing snap and hangman and reading when she dozed. At eleven o'clock Sonja rang the ship's bell outside the back door and I went to collect a tray of milk and biscuits which Caro and I shared while we listened to the sputtering of the mower in the top garden. At twelve o'clock the young gardener came down with a trug of salad; tomatoes not much bigger than the radishes, bright-green lettuce and knobbly cucumbers. Raspberries filled another basket. Still there was no sign of Jack and I knew that he didn't want to see me again.

Caro managed to hobble indoors for lunch. She couldn't bend her knee so we walked her backwards down the steps into the little pebbled garden outside the back door.

As we ate the raspberries with great dollops of clotted cream, our grandfather said, 'Got some business to see to in St Just this afternoon. Thought I'd take you and Jack with me, Isobel. Drop you off, pick you up later. Walk'll do you good.'

'I don't think Jack will want to come, Grand. He hasn't been round all morning and I don't think he'll come now.'

My grandparents looked at each other.

'Ah,' my grandmother said. 'Jack's been busy, Isobel, that's all. Avril was rather silly and borrowed something from the Town Hall yesterday and Jack has been doing his best to sort it out. He went for Eddy's bike too, but that had gone.'

I thought of Jack and Miss Avril in the garden. She had been dressed in a blazer, the over-long sleeves lapping her fingertips, the bright colours of the stripes making a moving, discordant patch in the pale, early light. Jack had been talking and gesturing and in my self-absorption I had thought he was talking about me, but now I saw it was of his wild-haired aunt he had been speaking, cajoling and reassuring. Poor, kind Jack.

Just before the end of lunch the telephone rang and Sonja came in and said quietly to our grandmother, 'It's Mrs Rocastle, ma'am, and she don't sound too happy.'

'That'll do, Sonja!' Our grandparents exchanged another look and I thought what a lot was being unsaid that day. She went into the hall. The telephone was in the passage to the kitchen so we could listen to one side of the conversation.

'A little shaken, of course, but she's much better today and being a sensible girl. No, I don't think it would be wise, she's resting at the moment. Isobel? Oh, I'm so sorry, Iris, but I've just sent Isobel out on an errand for me. No, absolutely not, it was an accident and no one was to blame. No, Iris, I really don't feel I could —' There was a longish pause here and then, 'No, it really isn't necessary. We're perfectly well able to manage and I have Sonja Hockin to help me.' Another pause and then our grandmother's voice again, 'If you wish. I'll see what I can arrange. You are quite sure it's a good idea, Iris? Very well then. Goodbye.'

When she came back into the dining-room her face was expressionless but her blue eyes were glittering with anger. I'd only seen her look like that a few times, usually connected with our grandfather's 'bits of business', and I held my breath, wondering what was to come. I looked across at Caro, who seemed as frozen with anticipation as I was. We weren't a bit afraid of our grandmother although I suspected that our grandfather was.

She said nothing for a few minutes and then, surprisingly calmly, 'Your mother sends you both her love and says that she and your stepfather will be coming to see you soon. She's asked me to book them into the Kings but says that she thinks your stepfather's niece, Ursula, is it, would be happier here with you.'

'But she's in America,' said Caro.

'She will be back for the last two weeks of the holidays and your mother and stepfather say that she would like to spend them with you in Cornwall, as you've told her so much about it.'

'I hate her. I hate her. I don't want her to come here and spoil things. Can't you say no, Gran?'

Our grandmother looked from Caro's agitated little face to me.

'What do you say, Isobel?'

I knew I couldn't say anything without crying. Ursula had taken my place as the eldest daughter in the home we shared in London and now she was going to come and take over here as well. She spoiled everything and I was desperate that my grandparents shouldn't be exposed to her flattery and guile. I knew too that once Jack had met her, he wouldn't any longer be interested in anyone as gauche and immature as I was then. How could I compete with Ursula's beauty and the deceptive insincerity of her words. She wanted everything of mine and now she was coming to Cornwall and the last of our secrets, mine and Caro's, would be plundered and taken back as her spoils to share with my mother. We would have no refuge left.

I didn't understand then, of course, that my grandparents had seen all this before, that they had known my mother for a long time and had watched, unable to help, while my father was driven out by my mother's frenetic and intense friendships with anyone she felt could augment and enrich her life.

I just looked at my grandmother, not able to answer her and it was my grandfather who said, 'So, that's the way the wind's blowing, is it? Knew there was something. Thought it was just this damned popish nonsense. Over to you, May, my dear.'

'Well, it's simply not possible to open the other

bedrooms, but I think we might perhaps put Ursula in the Old Nursery.'

Caro and I looked at each other in delight; she *did* understand. The room our grandmother meant was called the Old Nursery because it had bars across the window. It was marooned where there was a door and a small, separate landing, tucked under a corner of the stairs before they twisted upwards again to the attics. As long as we could remember no one had slept there and it was dark, with faded wallpaper and shutters over the barred windows. It had certainly never been a nursery and Caro and I believed that it had been the confine of some Cornish Mrs Rochester.

'Well done, May. The Old Nursery it is.' Our grandfather stood up and, so suddenly that it made all three of us jump, he brought his walking-stick down on the arm of a plump little ottoman with such violence that a cloud of dust spiralled like golden confetti in the light from the window.

'By God,' he roared, 'I won't have those little girls hurt any more,' and he marched into the hall shouting, 'HOCKIN, HOCKIN,' at the top of his voice.

Silence settled on the room again until my grandmother told me to get ready to go to St Just and I went reluctantly to wash and put on a clean shirt, still not convinced that Jack was as anxious to go as I was.

I was waiting for my grandfather in the porch, trying not to see the bleached skulls and horns twisted like corkscrews, that encircled it just above head height. Coming into the porch when the light was dim was always a terror, long spiky shadows thrown over the walls and floor.

I heard Jack before I saw him: the path to the front door was covered in small pebbles, as smooth and shiny as sucked butterscotch and even someone who walked as lightly as Jack gave some indication of his approach. As if he had been watching, my grandfather opened the door from the inner hall and joined me on the step. He was wearing a rose in his buttonhole, his silver hair glossy and thick, and I realised for the first time how handsome he was. I wondered if my father would look like him when he was old. He reached out his stick and tapped Jack lightly on the shoulder with the silver handle.

'Good boy, just in time. Wonderful day. Do us all good.'

I could see Hockin standing by the car and stared at him so that I wouldn't have to look at Jack. I had so badly wanted to see him and now I was too shy even to speak. My grandfather climbed into the front of the car beside Hockin so Jack and I had to sit together in the back.

My grandfather was right, it was a wonderful day. We drove up through Madron, the fields a dull orange where the barley stood waiting to be cut. Brambles scrambled over hedges where the ripe thistles waited only for a wind to send their down parachuting into the air. It was hot and very still. We could see cows waiting to move impatiently towards field gates, milking time not far off.

As we got nearer to Morvah the fields became smaller and rougher; croft fields, where here and there someone had cut the furze and moved the stones to make a field where corn was now growing. Later on, broccoli and turnips would struggle against the salty winds which shaved the tops off the landward-leaning trees. A mackerel sky spread inland from the sea, over great granite boulders too big to move, standing like monuments in the fields. Others looked as if they must overbalance and crash down the hills like a summer avalanche.

As we drove through almost empty lanes my grandfather pointed out a stand of Cornish elms, a patch of gorse flaming against a grey wall, two skewbald ponies in a yard: and we sang:

'My father was the keeper of the Eddystone
Light,
And he fell for a mermaid one fine night.'

'Stop at Boscaswell, Hockin. They can walk from there.' The car pulled off the road opposite a row of miners' cottages, the neglected front gardens showing which were the houses rented out to summer visitors. Jack and I got out of the car and my grandfather shouted through his window, 'Pick you up here at six o'clock,' and they were gone. Gone about the business for which my grandfather wore a yellow rose in his buttonhole and sang rude songs in his loud, deaf voice.

Jack and I turned down the narrow lane towards the sea. A tractor rumbled towards us and we pressed ourselves against the sticky escallonia hedge while it passed. Suddenly Jack took my hand and we began to run, dust flying from our feet, down towards the polished, turquoise water.

We walked hand in hand on the path along the cliff, leaving the Pendeen light behind us until we could see where the two old mines, the Crowns section Jack called them, perched like Merlin's castle over the sea and seemed to be floating in the air.

'We'll just go as far as Botallack today,' Jack said, 'another time we'll take the bus to Bank Square and start in St Just and walk to Cape Cornwall, if you like, or up to Ding Dong and we could go to Lands End and swim at Nanjizel. We'd have it all to ourselves, no one ever goes there as I don't think the visitors know how to get to it. There's an old cave on the beach where tin was dug out of the rocks.'

Jack stopped walking and looked at me. I could see a great herring gull, a golden aura around its body as it flew between us and the sun.

'There's so much we could do, Isobel,' he said and I noticed that Jack's strange eyes were the colour of the sea.

We left the path and sat on a grass-covered stone in a broken circle of stones around the centre of the abandoned dressing floor. There were two more mines away to our left and alone on Kenidjack cliff there was a white house, square on to the Atlantic. I was wondering what it would be like to live there in such isolation in the winter when Jack said, 'Imagine the wind hammering off the sea and the rain lashing against the windows.'

'How did you know what I was thinking?'

He smiled. 'I think it's a gift; I often know what people are thinking, more or less anyway. Actually I don't think anyone lives there now but I shall have a house like it one day. Somewhere on this cliff where I can walk every day and hear and smell the sea all the time. Do you think you would like that, Isobel?'

I thought about it for a while, not sure if it was the cliff or Jack that I wanted to be near.

'I think so. Perhaps a bit outside St Just, one of the little cottages, but on its own. I don't want to live near other people, I know that.'

He had been sitting gazing directly at the sea, which sparkled too fiercely for me to be able to look at it in comfort, and then he got up slowly and walked towards the edge of the cliff. The thrift was dry and dead but there were always a few fat, green cushions of leaves surrounding late flowers. Jack picked a small bunch, having to look hard for them.

'We'll buy two cottages, then, quite near each other and be friends for ever.' He gave me the sea pinks and I sat holding the little posy, happy as never before, in the sunshine, with Jack.

'My mother and I lived in St Just during the war, you know. My father was away in the army and my mother had an old cottage that had belonged to her grandparents, so we stayed there. We didn't have any money really but the aunts paid my school fees and made sure that we didn't starve.'

'I thought you said they didn't have any money.'

'Well, actually they've got rather a lot but they tend not to open letters from the bank. They seemed to manage better during the war, or perhaps my mother helped them, I don't really know. Anyway, it's all been sorted out now.'

'You are kind, Jack, the way you look after them. I watch you sometimes in the early morning and try to guess if it's going to be a good day or a difficult one.'

'I'm always aware of you watching,' he said, 'but I try not to let Aunt Avril know. She seems to need the morning air; it's a bit like letting a cat out, Aunt Clarrie doesn't like to hear her coughing, you see. If she knew you were watching, she might be shy.'

I could feel the velvety, grey-green stalks of the pinks in my hand and decided to press them under some of the heavier books in the library as soon as we got home. I knew they would fade and turn brown but I could always imagine the bold pink against that blue, blue sea and sitting with Jack while the sun stroked our skin with its golden hands.

We talked then as I'd never talked to anyone before, not even to Caro. We seemed to be the same age, me older than my actual years, made cautious and resilient by the difficulties I'd already overcome and Jack blithe but secretive.

I learned to lead him gently towards what I wanted to know, and to ask obliquely. If I was too bold in my questioning he would just smile at me and ask me something in exchange. I never then, or ever, heard him tell an outright lie but it was as if he had wrapped parts of himself in little pieces of secrecy and tied them with strings of mystery, like pass-the-parcel which we had all played at children's parties: layer after layer came off but, with Jack, you never seemed much nearer to the secret inside the wrappings.

He told me about his grandparents, how Jarvis Lemon had gone to America as a very young man and had married Beautiful Bella and brought her back to Cornwall. Clarrie and Avril were born only a year apart and Bella had a nursemaid called Gracie Jewell to help her with the two babies. When Bella died, Jarvis Lemon only waited six months before marrying Gracie, and their daughter, Jack's mother, was born the following year.

'We seem to specialise in joke names,' he said. 'Because my grandmother was called Jewell she called my mother Emerald, and because my father's name is Frost, everyone calls me Jack although it's not my real name at all, it's really Edmund. Edmund Jarvis Frost.'

Then I told him how I thought I should hyphenate my name to 'Bloody-Cuthbert' as my mother so often told me that I had the 'Bloody-Cuthbert ears' or the 'Bloody-Cuthbert hands' or, worse, that I was 'as deceitful as all the Bloody-

Cuthberts'. Knowing that he understood helped some of the pain to seep away like rain on thirsty earth.

I knew that Jack was only a few years older than me but it never occurred to me to doubt him. In the worst of the years that followed that lovely summer I never doubted the rightness of our friendship. I buried it deep in my heart where it formed part of the foundation of my life. Together with the unbreakable bond between Caro and me; the unconditional, deep love of our grandparents and the newer knowledge that God loved sinners and forgave the sin, to these I added Jack's love or friendship, whatever it was in those days, and it formed part of the bedrock through which my mother's taunts and barbs never quite managed to penetrate.

I knew I had to tell him about Ursula now that she was coming to stay. I was full of apprehension about their meeting and I tried not to think about it in case Jack *could* read my thoughts. I told him instead how I longed to have a room of my own so that Caro and I didn't have to share everything.

'The wardrobe and the chest of drawers are "ours",' I said, 'even the alarm clock and the wireless are "ours". We sleep together at school and we have no privacy at home either. She leaves her dirty handkerchiefs and apple cores on the bedside table and I'm so tidy that it drives her mad. It didn't matter when we were little but it does now, and we *could* have had a room each in the house but now my stepfather's niece, Ursula, is living with us and she's got a room to herself.'

I had spoken her name and now I must go on.

'You'll meet her soon as she's coming to stay for the last part of the holiday.'

'Is that what's worrying you, that this Ursula is coming down? We'll sort her out between us.'

'Oh! but you don't know her, Jack. She's *gorgeous,* everyone thinks so and she manages to make everyone believe she's dependable and clever and she's not, she's rather stupid really.'

I could feel a knot in my throat as if my dislike of Ursula was a physical object that was trying to choke me. Jack just looked at me and I stumbled on, 'She tells terrible lies and no one believes that what she says isn't true and she does things to get other people into trouble and when they do, you can just see that she's glad.'

I was almost crying now but I couldn't stop.

'She pretends to my mother that we're friends but I've heard her saying awful things about all of us and now she's coming down here and she'll do it all again and everything here will be spoilt. I hate her, Jack. I know it's a sin but I can't help it, I really do hate her.'

'Is that all?' he said.

I shook my head. He seemed to be taking it all so calmly that I decided to tell him the rest, the bit that I didn't really understand.

'There's something else, but I don't really understand it. It's a bit embarrassing but I'll tell you. My friend Regina, who knows lots of things, says,' I hesitated, 'well, that Father Ryan and Sister

Gabriel both love Ursula. I don't really understand what's wrong with loving someone, but I know it is from the way Regina said it.'

And sitting on the turf, with the shadow of the cliff stretching over the water as the sun started to sink, Jack explained to me what Regina meant and I understood for the first time what Reverend Mother meant by sins of the flesh.

He was still holding my hand and I sat thinking about what he had told me until he said, 'We'll have to go, Isobel, your grandfather will be back and he doesn't like to be kept waiting. Don't worry about Ursula any more, she sounds rather silly to me and you shouldn't be afraid of her.'

He stood up and pulled me to my feet and we walked back towards the cross roads, slowly this time with our feet scuffing in the sandy earth, reluctant to leave this place, which became for ever our own secret Eden.

10

And so the summer passed. Caro's leg healed but she seemed to have lost some of her boldness, some of the daring, which was so much a part of her character. She was happy to play with our cousins but said that her leg hurt if she rode the ponies. She gossiped with Sonja and spent hours with Clarrie Lemon, who seemed just as taken with her. She used to tell me what she'd learnt when we lay in bed in the warm summer night.

'Do you know, Bel, Sonja has two sisters and *three* brothers and they're *all* named after film stars. She's called after Sonja Henie and her sisters are called Faye and Gaynor. Faye and Gaynor are nicer than Alice and Janet, aren't they? Sonja's mum thinks so, anyway. Her brothers are called Eddy and Gil and Cary. Eddy's not called Edward but Nelson Eddy Hockin, isn't that wonderful? Gil is short for Gilbert, after John Gilbert, but the best is Cary. You'll never guess about him.'

'That's easy — Cary Grant.'

'Yes, but it's because Cary Grant's real name is Archibald Leach so the Hockins' Cary is named Archibald after Grand. It's a sort of puzzle but Sonja wouldn't tell me any more.'

One evening she told me that Miss Clarrie had let her try on all her jewels that afternoon.

'She's got boxes and boxes of them, Bel, and they're all *real.* She said she's going to leave me some when she dies. I hope it's her pearls, I like them best.'

She sighed happily and fell asleep before me as she always did and when I slept I dreamed of a grown-up Caro lying on a beach made up of rubies and sapphires, pearls and opals and emeralds. She was scooping them into little piles just as she did with the bits of weathered glass.

When we weren't on the beach or in the adjoining gardens we quite often went to our uncle's farm and Jack sometimes came with us. His aunts didn't seem to mind how much time he spent with us and when Caro sometimes stayed on the farm on her own for a few days, Jack and I took the bus or cycled to Newlyn or Chysauster and once to Hayle to watch birds on the mud flats. We talked about our next visit to St Just and decided to save it for the end of the holiday, something special to remember during the dark winter months. Separated by school we could remember the long sunny days together which belonged to the summer when I had emerged from the chrysalis of childhood and had tried with my still crumpled wings to join Jack who had already walked a little way along that path ahead of me.

The Old Nursery was cleaned and aired. Sonja washed the paintwork and carried away in a cardboard box the remains of a bird's nest which had fallen down the chimney, but nothing could really disguise the room's air of murky menace.

'My dear life,' Sonja said, 'your grandmother must dislike this Ursula some old lot to put her in here. I could easy have given a lick and a promise to one of the proper bedrooms instead of spending all day in here.'

'Gran's never met her, Sonja,' I said and Caro added, 'But we both hate her.'

'Well we shall have some fun then, I reckon. My dad says no one dislikes better than your gran.'

Caro and I were helping Sonja by making up the bed when Caro said, 'Sonja, do you know why there are bars across the window? Did anyone ever sleep in here?'

'I daresay, my bird.'

'You could ask your dad, Sonja, he'd know, wouldn't he?'

'Oh, he'd know right enough but sometimes it's better just to accept things as they are, Miss Caro, and not ask too much.'

We knew that was all we'd hear that day; when Sonja didn't want to gossip, no amount of wheedling, even from Caro, would persuade her.

Our parents were coming down by train and in the late afternoon Hockin took the car to meet them. We were waiting at home with our grandparents, tea ready in the garden, trepidation in my heart. It was a hot, thundery day, little flies biting and agitating, but cooler under the trees than in the house.

Caro, Jack and I had spent the morning swimming. The flies were less of a nuisance in the water but as soon as we came out and sat on the beach, clouds of little black insects flew out of the seaweed and settled on our sticky bodies. Caro and I were quarrelling in a desultory way, both, I suppose, conscious that the end of our freedom was near. I knew, and I thought that Caro knew, that much as we wanted to see our mother, the presence of Frank and Ursula would alter the way things had always been and I didn't want things altered, not quite yet. I wanted Frank, and particularly Ursula, to see that we weren't just two inconvenient children, but that we were important to other people, that we had opinions that were listened to and feelings that were respected.

'May, my dear, and Archie.' Our mother kissed the air near them both. 'This is Frank and here is Ursula, Frank's niece, and mine now too, of course.'

She looked around. 'Oh there you are. You look as if you've been running wild all summer. Really, Isobel, you look like a nigger and just look at your hair. Why can't you be tidy and well groomed like Ursula? Oh my God!' — suddenly she saw Caro's injured leg — 'What a ghastly scar. It'll never fade of course and she'll never be able to wear skirts that show her legs. You should have warned me how hideous it is, May.'

Until that moment Caro hadn't realised that her leg was ugly — and from that moment she never forgot it. The look of realisation on her face stayed in my mind's eye for days. Our grandfather put his arm around Caro and hugged her tightly to his side as he shook hands with Frank and Ursula. It had all started again and I felt the danger and familiar fear of loving my mother.

It was getting cooler and banks of black cloud were moving over the sea to the west when our parents left to walk to their hotel on the promenade. Soon we would have to show Ursula to her room and my grandmother decided to do it herself.

She led the way up the first flight of stairs, showing Ursula where Caro and I slept in our father's old bedroom and where the bathroom was that she was to use, before turning on to the back landing and opening the door to the Old Nursery. I was watching Ursula and I saw her teeth clench and I saw the look in her eyes but never, not by the slightest change of expression, did she give any other sign of what she thought of the awful little room.

The storm broke late in the evening and we ate our dinner of under-roast and runner beans from the garden while flashes of lightning lit up the room, bleaching the walls to an underwater-green. Crashing thunder followed each flash and the rumbles and threats lasted into the night.

We woke next morning to a day of translucent gentleness. The sky was a pale, soft blue, the air fresh and sweet. I was awake early and raised the blind on the window to look for Jack and his aunt in the garden. There was a tap on the door and

Ursula came in. I let the blind down and put my finger to my lips, showing her that Caro was still sleeping.

Ursula sat on my bed. 'What were you looking at, Isobel?' she whispered.

'Just seeing if the storm did much damage. Gran's opening the garden for the Deep Sea Firemen next week and she wants it to be at its best.'

'You mean Deep Sea *Fisher*men.'

'No, I don't.' Ursula didn't understand.

'Grand always calls them Firemen and *we* do too,' Caro's voice came from her bed.

I wanted Ursula to go, to leave me alone to imagine Jack and Miss Avril in their secret, early morning garden; Jack aware of whether or not I was watching, Miss Avril mourning over the damaged petals scattered, like her borrowed treasures, for anyone to walk on.

Caro got up and quietly we let ourselves out of the house; it was Sunday and we were all going to early Mass. Our grandfather was so opposed to our conversion that no matter what the weather he made us walk to church although it was a good distance from the house and uphill all the way. We passed the little Wesleyan chapel where Caro and I used to go to Sunday School, where there had been books of coloured stamps given for good attendance and a feast in the summer.

Frank met us at the door of the church.

'Where's Mummy?' Caro asked and Frank said that she was tired after the journey and was having a lie in. He found four seats together in the ugly pews, shiny with varnish like thick treacle.

'Introibo ad altare Dei,' the priest began and I tried to concentrate but with a heavy heart for I knew the time when Ursula would meet Jack was getting near.

Our mother and Frank were to lunch with our grandparents and when the roast beef had been cleared away, Sonja brought in a large blue bowl of junket peppered thickly with nutmeg and a smaller bowl of deep-yellow cream. There were some late redcurrants on a glass plate, but even the beauty of the food couldn't disperse the mood at the table. It was edgy and difficult, Caro and I more subdued than we'd been for weeks. Ursula praised everything and asked questions of my grandmother about the Garden Open Day.

After lunch Caro and I were told to take Ursula for a walk while everyone rested and our grandmother wrote her letters. Ursula didn't want to go to the beach so we walked reluctantly through woods where the first yellow leaves of the end of summer were appearing. Fat blackberries grew in abundance and I wished we'd brought a basket with us. At this time of the year everything seemed to me to be tired and ready to rest. The grassy verges of the roads were brown and the scarlet-berried hawthorn bushes covered in pale dust thrown up by passing cars. Seedheads and downy thistles stood where bluebells and anemones had shone in the spring. I thought of the sharp, spicy smell of nettles after rain and the smell of coconut from hot gorse bushes on the cliffs and I didn't want to share any of this secret, lovely world with Ursula.

Caro looked at me with an expression on her face that I knew meant mischief.

'We shouldn't be in these woods really, Ursula. A man has escaped from the loony bin and he does *awful* things to girls if he catches them. Sonja told me.'

Ursula said quite calmly, 'If that's true we'd better stick together and walk back to the road, but I shouldn't believe everything Sonja tells you, Caro, she doesn't look the kind of person I'd want to believe.'

'She's my best friend and she's nicer than you,' Caro shouted, 'and she does tell the truth, she does.'

With anyone else this childish bickering would have rumbled on for a while like a distant thunderstorm, and then been forgotten in the sunshine that followed, but with Ursula it was different and I knew what Caro wanted, so we both started to run through the trees, along paths familiar to us but unknown to Ursula. When we reached the road Caro ran on down the hill bordered with old palm trees, past escallonia and tamarisk, and slipped into the top garden by a small door hidden in the ivy on the wall.

I was frightened of what would happen if we both arrived home without Ursula and half frightened, too, of Sonja's story of the escaped lunatic. What if he had found Ursula alone in the wood and had done to her whatever it was he did to girls. I was resting from the run along the dark paths and vacillated between my desire to leave Ursula to find her own way back to my grandparents' house and the prodding of my conscience to go back and find her, when I saw her coming towards me along the stony path that crossed a little stream before it left the wood behind.

There was something so steely in her self-control that for the first time in the year I had known her, my dislike and antipathy towards her was touched with real fear. I wanted to run, like Caro, back to the safety of our grandparents' garden, where there were real people, and not to be alone with this beautiful, cold creature who said softly, 'That was a silly thing to do, Bel. I shan't forget it.'

We walked back in silence and found everyone sitting in the shade of the catalpa tree, long black beans hanging from the branches where the chestnut-like flowers had blossomed in the spring, leaves fluttering in the slightest breeze.

It was a hot, still day and deck chairs and rugs were set out on the grass. My grandfather was trying his best to keep awake but his conversation was more abrupt than ever as he struggled not to slip into the abyss of sleep.

'I went to see The Girls this morning,' said my mother, 'they seem madder than ever.'

My grandmother said nothing and my mother went on, 'Frank thought they were mad too, didn't you, Frank?'

'Well, I wouldn't say *mad* exactly, Iris.'

'That isn't what you said this morning. I've heard that Avril has been stealing again,' she went on. 'How does she get away with it, May? Anyone else would be in prison by now but those two, just because they are who they are, get away with anything. I suppose that boy helps them.'

'Oh yes, Jack helps them a good deal,' said my grandmother, 'they'll miss him when he has to go back to school. Just as we shall miss Isobel and Caroline. It's been *such* a joy to have them here for the holidays.' She was drawing my mother's attention away from danger, deliberately misunderstanding her reference to Jack.

It didn't work then, any more than it ever did. My mother continued, her high voice reaching quite far enough to be heard by Avril and Clarrie, where they were turning the corner of the wall that divided the two houses and were starting to walk up the path towards us. She tried something else.

'Have you been out alone with Jack, Isobel?'

I could feel the blush starting in the pit of my stomach and spreading through every fibre of my body and knew that Ursula was watching me keenly. I didn't have to answer before my mother continued, 'well, I shouldn't think you'd come to much harm going out with that pansy boy.'

She gave a small, tight laugh and looked at Frank who pretended to be shocked and said, 'Oh, Iris, you shouldn't say things like that,' but he laughed in a way that encouraged her.

'Oh here they come' — as if she'd just noticed

them — 'put your cigarette case away, Frank, or she'll have that too. *Whatever* do they look like.'

Clarrie and Avril had reached the circle of chairs as she said this and it was impossible for them not to have heard her. I felt sick with embarrassment and shame. I saw to my surprise that Avril was wearing a frock and high-heeled sandals. It didn't suit her at all: she looked much better in her usual old jodhpurs and her father's big shirts. Clarrie was dressed in cream tussore. She had a long double row of pearls and a feathered comb in her hair. Her shoes were of pale glacé kid with the heels worn down to ragged stumps. My grandmother stood up, her eyes glinting.

'Come and sit down, my dears. Sonja will bring tea and as you enjoy it, I thought we'd have it iced today, it's so refreshing.'

My mother's expression hardened. She knew it was a move to exclude her.

'Not for me, thank you, May. Frank won't have iced tea either. We like a proper cup of tea in the afternoon.'

She bit her upper lip and I saw the danger signal. She turned to Avril.

'So unusual to see you in a frock, Avril, and how *nice* you look, my dear, you should dress like that more often.'

The two sisters settled into the old upright deck chairs and Frank asked where Jack was.

'Jack?' said Clarrie as if she wondered whom he meant. 'Oh Jack. Yes, he'll be along when he's finished whatever it is he's doing.' I looked at Clarrie in admiration. She had foiled them.

My mother said, very sharply, 'Caroline, come and sit by me where I can watch you, and leave Clarrie alone.'

Caro had been examining a large amethyst ring, slipping round and round on her friend's thin finger.

I wanted to get Avril away from danger so I said to her, 'Would you like to see the peaches, Miss Avril? They're absolutely splendid, Grand says. He's going to put them in the Show.'

'Oh, absolutely splendid,' said my mother in a mocking voice, 'really, Isobel!' Miss Avril put down her empty glass and together we walked up the granite steps to the top garden. As we were looking at the ripening fruit nestling along the grey wall, Jack suddenly appeared and dropped down beside us. He only had to look at my face to see what was going on.

'Oh Jack,' I said, 'be careful,' and we all knew I didn't mean about jumping over the wall.

'I hear your parents are coming back to live in Cornwall, Jack,' my mother said. 'Is your father out of prison then?'

There was a deathly silence and even Frank must have known that she'd gone too far. Jack looked at my mother and said quietly, 'I'm afraid I don't quite understand, Mrs Rocastle.'

'Well, that's where he's been, isn't it? I know no one likes to say so, but' — I mean — where else could he have been?

Jack looked at her for a moment and then said,

'My father, Mrs Rocastle, has been in a psychiatric hospital. Perhaps you didn't know that he was a prisoner-of-war of the Germans for three years and when he came home he had a nervous breakdown. If you had asked me, I would have told you, so that you wouldn't have needed to make something up to explain his absence.'

I was terrified for Jack; he hadn't heeded my warning at all and now I held my breath knowing how my mother treated anyone who contradicted her but it was as if she hadn't heard a word that Jack had said and to my bewilderment she turned to my grandfather.

'If you're going to the abattoir tomorrow, Archie, Frank would like to go with you.'

All this time Ursula had been sitting silently on the edge of the circle. It wasn't in her nature to be self-effacing and there was a deliberate, calculated stillness in her façade that drew everyone's eye to her. She was wearing one of her American dresses of dull orange that shimmered to gold as the sun sent little sparks of light dancing from it. A black velvet ribbon held back her beautiful dark-red hair in a low bunch, except for a few fronds which had broken free and lay softly around her face. She looked serene and beautiful and I ached with jealousy.

Ursula had come back from San Francisco with a suitcase full of new clothes chosen by her mother whose flair for the dramatic had found an unexplored territory to work on in her almost unknown daughter. Ursula had circular skirts made with yards of material that spun from her little waist, jackets with a frilled peplum, pedal pushers and swinging jackets to match. There were dresses and shirts the colour of strawberry and coffee ice-cream and red and green plaids and blue denim jeans. The two best linen dresses — the one she was wearing today and another that reminded me of a mallard's neck, iridescent blue and green as she turned — fitted closely to her body, and with everything she wore flat leather pumps that looked like my ballet shoes. She had these in various colours, with pretty, boxy handbags to match.

Contrasted with our old Aertex shirts and let-down summer dresses, the faded hemline disguised with ric-rac braid, she looked like an alien bird, like the ones who visited Scilly on their migratory flights each year.

Later, Caro and I sat, as we so often did, watching Sonja in the kitchen while she rolled pastry to cover a blackberry and apple pie. It was so hot that the window, which reached almost to the floor, was open and I could see the bright-green patches of duckweed growing on the stones where water from the drain splashed over so that even in the driest weather this hidden part of the garden was shadowy and cool. There were ferns here too, and mosses dark and velvety, and sometimes Sonja would take a kitchen chair outside and read her *Cornishman*, sitting in the shade.

I knew she was watching me but she said nothing. Caro was shaping apples and leaves out of left-over pastry and Sonja put the little grey shapes on top of her pie before painting them all over with egg yolk.

'I think Ursula's like an exotic bird. A Bird of Paradise,' I said at last, wanting to hear what the words sounded like, said out loud.

' 'Es, a bird all right, Miss Isobel, a proper cuckoo in the nest that one is.' She turned her head, smiling at me and added, 'Don't 'ee take no notice of she, my 'andsome,' knowing that I enjoyed hearing her talk in her familiar idiom.

'One thing's for sure,' she added, 'Master Jack wasn't impressed by her so you needn't fret on that score.'

I didn't pretend to Sonja not to know what she meant, she had been party and chandler to too many of my expeditions with Jack to be taken in, but Sonja, always watchful and intelligent, had seen my fear dissolve as Ursula's vigilant charm seemed wasted on Jack. He was polite to her but nothing more; I saw none of the will to please her that I was used to from girls in the convent; no spark seemed to be ignited by her beauty and her contradictory stillness that drew so much attention to her, drew Jack no more than anyone else.

As my anxiety over their meeting lessened it was replaced by another, sharper fear. She had been profoundly angry when Caro and I had left her in the woods, I knew her well enough to see that, and I waited tensely for the repercussions.

We were to have lunch early the next day as the garden would be open from two o'clock and we were all to help in serving teas. We were eating cold meat and salad when my grandfather suddenly said to me, 'Want you to drive the car this afternoon, Isobel. Hockin's got to help with this damn-fool garden thing and I need a driver.'

I thought it was one of our jokes but when I looked at him I saw that he was quite serious.

'Don't be so foolish, Archie. Isobel can't drive, she's much too young.'

'Only got to change gear, I'll steer. Can't stay here with my blasted house overrun by nosy parkers.'

'You know I want you here. Everyone expects to see you.'

'They'll be disappointed then. Bit of business to see to in Madron. Can't stand it, watching them stealing cuttings and trampling in the flower beds trying to look in at the windows. They're to use the gardeners' lavatory, May, won't have them in the house.'

We knew he had made up his mind to go out and that our grandmother was equally determined that Hockin should stay and help her. She didn't really need him but this was an annual tussle, a trial of strength between them, and our grandfather would arrive home later with a bucket of crabs or a new plant for the garden which she would refuse to accept until he had apologised.

'Isn't there anyone else you could ask, Mr Cuthbert? What about Uncle Frank?'

We all looked at Ursula; she didn't know the rules of this game and our grandfather didn't bother to answer, but with an exaggerated limp he walked to the telephone in the kitchen passage and called Neil Williams, who always drove him on Hockin's day off. He managed to make his escape just before the first of the visitors arrived.

I wished I could have escaped as well. I hated it when everyone with half a crown to spare could invade our garden, criticising and comparing it with their own. My grandmother had gratified her passion for dead-heading her flowers with rigour, and the gardeners had weeded and raked, edged and trimmed until every corner looked like a picture on a calendar.

> Peshawar Lodge, the gracious home of Mr and Mrs Archibald Cuthbert, was once again the venue for a Garden Open Day held in aid of the Fund for the Relief of Deep Sea Fishermen. The many people who willingly paid half a crown to see the resplendent display of flowers from around the world which grow so abundantly in this favoured corner of Arthur's Realm, were not disappointed.
>
> Cornish Cream Teas were served most charmingly in a tranquil corner by Mr and Mrs Cuthbert's granddaughters and their friends.
>
> Unfortunately Mr Archibald Cuthbert was unable to be present, having a bit of business to see to in Madron.

'Oh Jack, it doesn't say that. Let me see.'

I snatched Sonja's *Cornishman* from him. We were sitting in the little room between the kitchen and the boot-room where my grandmother did the flowers. We shared a wide, slate window-seat and read the *Cornishman* in the dim light from the window next to the sink.

There were copper and brass watering cans on the shelves above the sink and on the wall opposite the window was an old wooden dresser, heaped with my grandmother's vases and bowls; chipped china and old silver stored together in a kaleidoscopic jumble. There were baskets on the floor and in the dresser drawers she kept string and scissors and plasticine. It was almost always cool in the little room and it smelled of old flower water and damp moss.

It was in here during the previous afternoon that my grandmother had taken off her watch before crushing the ends of some late-flowering, long-stemmed roses and plunging them into a jug of cold water. She had changed her everyday man's watch with its wide, leather strap for her best one of platinum and diamonds which our grandfather had given her at about the same time as Cary Hockin had been born. She put the tall enamel jug on the window-seat to await the winner of the raffle and, seeing Clarrie Lemon framed in the dingy little window looking lost and fragile, she had hurried outside to talk to her.

Miss Clarrie was wearing her best garden party clothes. Her hat was a pale-grey straw, rather shredded around the edges but beautiful, with roses and pansies of faded silk encircling the brim. She wore a pale-grey lace jacket, as precisely delicate as a cobweb, over a silvery, pleated dress which swung like a bell as she walked in her little cuban-heeled shoes over the manicured grass. She looked so alluring in her beautiful, threadbare clothes that it had made my throat tighten just to look at her and I understood very well why Caro wanted to protect her from the ridicule of people who didn't understand.

Miss Avril had arrived rather later than her sister and there were nudges and covert smiles as she appeared. I was glad that she had abandoned her dress as she looked distinguished and striking wearing white cricket flannels and a striped shirt. I felt a frisson of anxiety however, as I saw that she was carrying the crocodile handbag and I determined to stay as close to her as I could. Most people, once they had walked around the gardens, decided to sit down in the shade for a cup of tea and I had no time to watch over Miss Avril as Caro and Jack and I ferried relays of trays which Ursula and Sonja in the kitchen were filling with scones and cream and cups of tea.

It wasn't until a delighted Mrs Williams, mother of Neil, was announced as winner of the raffle and my grandmother went to collect her roses from the house, that she remembered taking off her watch. The shelf above the sink now bore only the watering cans.

No one had seen the watch; no one who shouldn't have been there had been seen in the flower-room, but the watch was missing. I felt taut with apprehension every time I thought of the crocodile handbag and couldn't even talk to Caro about it: I didn't want the words to be out in the open air. In some bizarre way I felt that just as Caro loved Miss Clarrie, I was responsible for Miss Avril and I couldn't bear for her to have taken my grandmother's watch, it was too particular, too intimate a part of her.

Dinner that evening was a tense and dismal affair. It was to have been a treat, fish and chips for everyone so that Sonja could have the evening off. My grandmother, surprisingly, seemed to be the one least affected by the loss. She didn't like the watch but wore it, I think, as a warning to my grandfather when she was cross with him. She was angry though that he had been proved right about leaving the house open, but he said very little and ate heartily.

It was my mother who reiterated over and over the same theme.

'What do you expect, May? Avril was prowling around in the house, I saw her myself, and she certainly couldn't resist a bauble like that. Why not just go and ask her. Just go and say that you want your watch back. We all know she's got it. Why don't you just go and ask her.'

On and on until I could feel tears filling my eyes and Caro's foot touched mine under the table, neither of us daring to say a word. I loved fish and chips but these seemed cold and greasy and disgusting.

Suddenly our grandfather flung down his napkin, 'I won't have this, Iris, do you hear? Avril would never borrow anything personal of May's, don't you *understand* that?'

My mother smiled at him.

'Oh, I understand very well, Archie. I understand about the watch very well, believe me. I've often thought how odd it was that you decided to give May such a lavish present, just about the time that Evie Hockin had her little Cary, wasn't it? Very odd really. Don't you think so, Frank?'

Frank couldn't ignore her question but he looked fairly embarrassed and protested, 'Hush, Iris, that's enough.'

Surprisingly, my mother did stop but the look on her face frightened me. Before long, I thought, she'll start blaming me for whatever it is that is being implied in the silence and tension of this meal, and the fear-filled years that had been smudged and smoothed over by my grandparents flooded back with a sharpness that made me feel weak.

I was trying not to understand what my mother had just said and jumped when Ursula's glass of orange squash seemed to slip out of her fingers and a creeping yellow stain splashed across the white damask.

'I'm so sorry, Mrs Cuthbert. I'll fetch a cloth,' and she went into the kitchen. When she came back with a rag, there was something in her left hand. She walked to my grandmother's place and laid the little, sparkling watch beside her on the table.

'This is very difficult and I hardly know what to say because I wouldn't want you to think I was accusing Sonja, but when I was looking for a clean cloth, I opened the drawer in the kitchen table as I thought that was where they were kept, and I couldn't help seeing the watch.'

Ursula looked hesitant and embarrassed; it was one of her better performances and even I, just for a fleeting moment, almost believed her.

'I'm sure that Sonja must have put it there to keep it safe for you, in case anyone *did* wander into the house, but she must have gone off and forgotten to tell you where it was. Anyway, you've got it back now and I'm sure it was all a mistake.'

'Yes, you're quite right, Ursula, it is a big mistake.' My grandmother's face was white with anger and I hoped that she never looked at me in the way in which she was now looking at my cousin. She put the watch into her pocket and I never saw it again but that year's cheque to the Deep Sea Fishermen was for an unprecedented amount.

While we helped my grandmother to clear the table and make coffee and my grandfather fetched cigars from the morning-room, my mother and Frank talked together but too quietly for me to hear what they were saying. As soon as we were all sitting round the table again she said, 'Frank and I have decided that we will go home at the end of this week and not wait until next weekend as we'd planned. I'm grateful to you, May, for putting up with the girls all these weeks but I think it's time we all went home.'

Neither Caro nor I liked coffee very much but we were drinking it tonight, white and sweet, unlike Ursula who pretended to like hers black and without sugar. Caro's cup smashed down on the saucer.

'We can't go, the holiday's not over yet. It's the R-R-Regatta next week and we're going on Gil Hockin's boat as M-M-Mermaids.'

'No, my lady, you're not; you're coming home with us. I think you've seen quite enough of the Hockins and your precious Clarrie Lemon for one summer.'

Caro started to cry.

'Tell her, Bel, tell her we c-c-can't go yet, we've got another w-w-week and I've got to say goodbye to the ponies and it's the Regatta and — everything.'

She sobbed desperately but our mother just looked at her and said, 'Stop that nonsense at once, Caroline. You'll do as you are told and if this is the way you behave when I let you go away on your own I'll never let you come down here again.'

The fondness between Miss Clarrie and Caro was not lost on my mother and she felt that affection due to her was being squandered on someone else and she was determined to stop it.

Our grandmother turned to me.

'Will you and Caroline and Ursula do something for me?'

I nodded.

'Will you go round the garden one more time to see if there is anything lying about and make a note of what has to be done tomorrow?'

I don't know what was said in the dining-room while we uselessly patrolled the garden but when we came back into the house, our parents had left and my grandmother told us that we would be staying on for the whole of our promised holiday. Her eyes were red and our grandfather was very sweet to her and almost quiet for a change.

When she came to kiss us goodnight we sat for a long time, while the moon threw a pale disguise over the room and our night-lights flickered, but we didn't talk very much. Eventually Caro fell asleep and then my grandmother talked about things that afterwards I never told anyone, and never Caro or Jack.

'Grand and I know things are difficult, my darling child, but you must be brave and try to help Caro, she hasn't your strength, Isobel. You're very like me and we can endure and usually find something amusing in the worst of situations.'

She sat for a while, holding my hand and then said in a more everyday voice, 'Now, I'm going to tell you something that you can tell Caroline when the time comes: Grand has decided to leave you both some money — he calls it your Running Away Fund — and it is to help you to do whatever *you* want when you are older.'

She told me too what I needed to know, that my father loved us but that he couldn't stay with us.

'Your mother has lots of good points, Isobel, but she has been very spoiled all her life and she has never learned to share or to make allowances for other people. I don't know if you know that she was born when your grandparents had given up hoping for a child: they'd been married for twenty years, you know, and then your grandfather died when your mother was only ten months old and your grandmother had to bring her up on her own and she really had no idea how to go about it, so your mother managed to get her own way in everything. When you always get what you want, you soon find that nothing is ever good enough and when people disappoint you because you expect too much of them, then things get very difficult.

'Your mother really needs someone to stand up to her and not to give in to her all the time. That's why she won't argue with Grand — and did you notice how she ignored Jack when he corrected her about his father — but sadly she usually manages to bully the nicest people because they won't answer her back. I suppose it makes her feel that she is still able to get her own way with someone but it doesn't do, you know, and just brings unhappiness all round.

'I feel sorry for your stepfather, but that's none of my business and you *are.*'

We sat for a while in silence and then she said,

'When you're older you'll understand these things better, but there are marriages which last even if to other people they seem odd, and others which break where the man and woman seem perfectly well suited. I don't really understand it myself,' she said, 'but I think it has something to do with real love, with wanting what is best for someone else, even if it means having to swallow your pride and hide your pain. Something like that anyway.'

She was still holding my hand in her own square, little hands and I was safe and loved.

'Gran, there's something I've never said out loud and if I do, you won't ever tell, will you?'

'Of course I won't.'

'Caro and I don't like Frank very much and we didn't want to have to be Catholics and it's not fair, any of it, and Ursula's the worst of all.'

'There I agree with you, Isobel, but I fancy your mother may have revised her opinion of Ursula a little today.'

'You mean about the watch? How *could* she, how *could* she. First they blamed Miss Avril and then Sonja and it was that vile Ursula all the time. You knew it, didn't you, Gran?'

'I did, but I wasn't aware that you did.'

'I saw her spill her drink deliberately and she's always doing things like that to get other people into trouble but Mummy and Frank believe everything she says.'

'Mmmm, perhaps, but your mother is a very shrewd woman, you know. She understands just how to exploit people's weaknesses and Ursula is a weapon she can use to her own advantage.'

'That's just what Jack said.'

'Well then, if Jack and I both said it, it *must* be true! You've made one very good friend this summer, haven't you?'

'Three, I think. Jack and Miss Avril and Sonja. It's funny, isn't it, how sometimes you just *know* when a person is sound.'

'Did Grand tell you that? "Sound" is his highest form of praise. He's sound, even if not everyone knows it,' and all at once I understood that my doughty little grandmother was herself afraid of my mother; afraid of the damage that her half-understood, half-certain innuendoes could inflict, the mischief caused by her malign allusions undermining the image that my grandparents presented to the world.

She must have stayed with me until I fell asleep as I don't remember her leaving but in the morning there was still a trace of lily of the valley in the room, as insubstantial as a dream.

11

1950

The letters were given out early on Saturdays and we were dressed in our outdoor clothes, ready to follow on foot the first hunt of the season. The autumn had been very cold and dry and frost was sparkling and turning the trees into outdoor echoes of the tracery that decorated the ceiling of the town's sixteenth-century abbey.

As we walked along the rides, leaves crunched under our wellingtons and our breath was pale as smoke. Sometimes a pheasant's cackle came from the woods as we left the trees behind and walked on the frozen ridges of a ploughed field towards the village from where the horses would start.

The de Maides rattled about in a house that had been built soon after the defeat of the Spanish Armada. Now, four hundred years later, Sir Neville, Lady Felice and their four daunting children lived in one wing which was in much less good repair than their stables, and it was here that the Meet was gathering.

I'd met them several times when I'd been staying with Patsy and was very shy of Sir Neville. He liked to tease the girls he met, knowing that most of them would imagine themselves to be in love with him, and he was a man whom gossip followed. Like all the de Maides he was very tall, with a tanned, lined face and black hair brushed close to his head. He had knowing brown eyes and the strong, bowed legs of a horseman and I wanted to dislike him because he made me think of things I knew to be sinful.

I hoped he wouldn't see me as I looked for Patsy and Mary Clare among the riders in front of the shabby, handsome old house. I didn't really want to talk to anyone, but to lose myself in the exertion of following hounds as far as we could, before returning, exhilarated and mud-spattered, to the convent.

There was no mud that November though, the ground was frozen hard already and I thought about my grandfather and wondered how they had buried him. In my pocket was the letter addressed to Caro and me together which I had collected soon after breakfast. It was from Frank and I hadn't yet had a chance to give it to Caro. I wanted to break it to her more gently than Frank had been able to do. I felt sorry for him, having to do it at all, but then I felt sorry for Frank a lot of the time these days.

Dear Isobel and Caroline,
Your mother has asked me to let you know the sad news about your grandfather. I'm sorry to tell you that he died three weeks ago —

Three weeks! Three weeks in which we still thought he was alive and going about his bits of business: three weeks when our little grandmother must have wondered why we didn't write to her. I had turned back to Frank's letter:

> It was too far for us to go to the funeral, of course, but your mother sent flowers from all of us and says to tell you that you are lucky girls as he has left you both a tidy sum.

I was cold when we lost the horses and turned back for the convent and it wasn't until late in the afternoon that I found Caro, practising the piano. Since the accident to her leg two years ago she had ridden hardly at all and now she disapproved of hunting altogether.

When she'd read Frank's letter I said, 'Shall we go to Chapel and pray for him?'

She shrugged her shoulders. 'You can if you like but he's been dead for three weeks, what good's it going to do?'

'It might, if he's in purgatory. We might get him out a bit quicker.'

'You don't really have to believe all that nonsense, you know, Bel. I just hope Grand's up there seeing about his bits of business just like he always did,' and, after a pause, 'I wonder how much he's left us.'

'Why do you think they didn't tell us for three weeks — so we couldn't write to Gran?'

'They are awful, aren't they, but Gran will understand.'

She sat looking down at her hands in her lap and then said, very softly, 'I wish we could run away, Bel, and live alone like Miss Clarrie and Miss Avril and no one could tell us what to think and make out that we're going to hell if we just make a mistake. And we'd never have to go to confession and make ourselves so frightened all the time.' She started to cry. 'Poor old Grand. I hope he died doing something wicked and that he was happy doing it.'

I thought it quite likely, but I knew how much she had loved him and I didn't know how to help her so sat on the uncomfortable chair beside the piano until she stopped crying.

'Gran told me that Grand called the money the Running Away Fund and it's for us to be able to do whatever we want with it, so he did know how you feel.'

'Nobody knows how I feel, how can they.' She pounded the keys of the piano in a pandemonium of noise until the door was flung open and Mother Celestia stood there. A cold draught rushed in with her from the corridor, dispelling the warmth built up in the little music-room.

'I didn't know you'd graduated to Schoenburg, Caroline.'

Mother Celestia had arrived at Stella Maris at the same time as Mother Michael, as if some sympathetic fate had diluted the ferocity of one nun with the gaiety of the other. Mother Celestia was the only nun I had ever seen who threw back her head and laughed as if she meant it. She was six feet tall and as black as jet.

She saw Caro's tears and the letter lying in her lap.

'I think you'd better tell me what's wrong, Isobel.'

'We've just heard that our grandfather is dead, Mother.'

'That must be a great sadness to you, I'm sure. We'll include him in our evening prayers tonight and you could make a Novena to Our Lady for the repose of his soul.' Then, briskly, 'Now dry your eyes, Caroline, and hurry in to tea, you don't want a detention for being late.'

She didn't need to tell us that it was self-indulgent to show our grief, it was a lesson we had already learned and if we were to mourn it had to be done secretly. This was a lesson that others too had to learn in the following weeks.

I had come to hate 'You're the Cream in my Coffee' almost as much as the music of *Les Sylphides.* We had progressed to ballroom dancing on Sunday evenings now but unless someone could be persuaded to play the Valeta or the St Bernard's Waltz we danced to Victor Sylvester, the same two records played over and over, on the new gramophone.

The record started again but I didn't want to dance any more. I'd spent the whole day rehearsing *Les Sylphides* for the Christmas concert and my legs ached so much I decided to see if Matron would give me some liniment so I left the Hall and crossed the corridor, intending to go up the back stairs. There was a small room at the top of the stairs where hot bottles and breakfast trays had been prepared when the house was still in use by the last family who had lived in it. Sister Infirmarian of the dead-grey hands had been replaced by an ex-Wren, intent on proving that cold water and sarcasm cured most ills. On Sunday evening she supervised the hair-washing of the younger girls in this small infirmary, so I knew where to find her.

The back stairs stood at the convergence of three passages and there was no one about as I walked tiredly down the longest of the corridors. There was only one light on and I walked in shadow near the walls so I'm sure that Ursula didn't see me as she slipped, as silent as I, across the end passage and, as silently, let herself out by the back door. She wasn't furtive but her swift, silent movement was secretive and I wondered for a moment if I had imagined seeing her at all, but I knew I hadn't imagined seeing stars against a black sky and I did remember that very clearly; and the way the door closed silently against the starry blackness. I hoped that I imagined, though, the figure blacker than the wall against which it stood: afterwards I was sure that I hadn't.

I woke very early the next morning, disturbed by a small noise in the dormitory. I lay quietly and saw Mother Clare whispering to Stella, who got up, dressed and crept out of the room. I knew it was only six o'clock because just as she closed the door I heard the Angelus bell ringing.

That morning Mass was said by Father Abdale, the priest who had taken Father Ryan's place at the old convent. I wanted to ask where Stella had gone but I couldn't see Mother Clare anywhere and Mother Michael's cold, tight face brooked no questions.

At the end of a subdued breakfast she rang the brass bell for silence.

'There is to be a special Assembly this morning. Make your beds as quickly as possible and instead of taking your usual exercise outside you are to go straight to the Hall. You will keep silence from this moment and you are all on your honour to obey.'

She said Grace in a distracted way and we walked silently upstairs. I knew now that something was terribly wrong and that Ursula and Father Ryan were somehow involved. Since Mother Michael had come to the convent two years ago to replace Mother Patrick, it was she who had come to dominate our lives; her cold, humourless personality and cruel sarcasm bringing with them an unease, a distrust, that seeped and filtered through our days. I don't believe there was anyone who wasn't afraid of her to some degree.

Everything about Mother Michael was pale: pale-grey eyes, pale, thin lips and a face that, even in the heat of summer, stayed as pale as milk.

When she was angry two red patches, quite round, like a face in a child's painting, burned on her cheeks, and her thin nose looked as if someone had pinched and bruised the flesh on either side of it.

She knew that all her girls were a seething mass of lust and that it was her duty to destroy any affection and warmth between them, for if girls couldn't control their feelings towards one another, what would happen when they were without the restraints she placed on them in the convent and they were exposed to men. She kept us in subjugation because she knew it was for our salvation, warmth and human emotion crushed and branded as sin, while fear and deceit flourished as the decree of a loving God.

Perceptible apprehension was all around us when we gathered in the Hall in front of what seemed to be the whole Community. Even Mother Bernard, who usually spent her time reading and dozing quietly these days was there, but I still couldn't see Mother Clare. A few coughs, hastily smothered, as Mother Michael had told us that coughing and sneezing were vulgar and could always be controlled by will power; a soft shuffling as we gathered in groups, and Reverend Mother clapped her hands for attention.

'Bonjour mes filles.'

'Bonjour, ma mère.'

'I have something very grave to tell you. Yesterday evening there was a road accident in the town and Mrs Lightowler who was well known to many of you as Stella's mother was, most unfortunately, killed.'

There was the sound of ninety indrawn breaths and Reverend Mother nodded to Mother Michael, who stepped forward to take her place.

'Father Ryan was,' she paused as if searching for the right word, 'present,' that was it, 'at the time of the incident and is presently helping the —' she paused again, 'the authorities. You will, of course, do all you can to help Stella when she returns to school and the best way to do that is not to talk about her mother's death and there will be *absolutely no discussion* of the circumstances of the accident. I shall know if my trust in you is broken.' Her eyes raked around the subdued groups of girls. 'Is that understood?

'Some of the day girls may have heard wild rumours in the town and I shall be talking to them separately later on, but in the meantime you will not discuss this among yourselves or with *anyone at all*, and that includes writing letters to your parents. Is that *perfectly* clear to everyone?'

'Yes, Mother Michael,' in unison like a sigh.

Mother Michael's face was tight and almost blue in its pallor. Her hands were tucked in her sleeves and I imagined them clasping her cold forearms like two burrowing animals hibernating for the winter. Some girls were crying; they weren't Stella's close friends and I wondered why they did it.

I felt sad and shocked, not just for my friend Stella but because I had liked Mrs Lightowler and now I felt ashamed of the times I had joined in the giggling comments about her brightly patterned carpets and her reproduction furniture. In our demonstration of superiority we pretended to offer each other drinks from a cocktail cabinet and mocked the pictures on her walls.

We knew, by some osmotic process, that it was the Lightowlers who had bought the gramophone to which we danced and who had paid for the new red velvet curtains for the stage. I remembered Stella's old dress that I had worn for my Reception into the Church and I suspected many other acts of kindness had emanated from the grey stone villa that stood on a hill overlooking the town.

Stella's grandparents had built the house and Stella's parents had modernised it, so that the grey exterior left you unprepared for the glossiness inside. Everything was modern and up to date; red and yellow and pale blue had replaced the maroon and beige which had been their parents' choice. The colours were too bright, the furniture too obviously new, but Stella's family fitted comfortably into their shiny carapace and were content and happy and found good in everything.

Stella was the only old-fashioned piece in the modern jigsaw of their lives. She was small and plump and her hazel eyes were calm, her skin smooth and creamy. She had small, graceful hands and feet and although not considered pretty by most people, she reminded me of a beautiful Jersey cow and I thought her lovely. After Caro and Jack and my grandmother, Stella was the person I loved most in the world. Her gentle manner misled people into overlooking her intelligence and although this sometimes worked to her advantage, she was far too perceptive not to understand that her beloved, jolly father was paying many times over for his daughters' entrance into a world which would otherwise always have remained closed to them. She was hurt but accepted pragmatically that the nuns patronised her parents, their soft local accent and conspicuous wealth the two components which both engaged and repelled those to whom all men should have been equal, but the convent needed more money than it had if it were to expand and Mr Lightowler had money.

Stella's sweet nature came equally from both her parents; she looked like her father but her intelligence came from her mother, and now that comfortable little figure was dead, crushed under the wheels of a car driven by a drunken priest one starry night as she went to post a letter. A priest, moreover, whom I felt certain I had seen standing in the dark as my cousin Ursula had moved silently across the yard to join him in the shadow of the wall, as she had so often before.

Stella came back to school a week later. The nuns made no concessions for her, it was as if she had been on holiday or absent through illness and they changed the subject if she spoke of her mother.

There was a bathroom at the top of the back stairs, stark and white in contrast to the sybaritic surroundings of the other bathrooms, and it was in this discouraging little room that Mother Michael carried out her nocturnal interviews and interrogations. There was nowhere to sit down and a deliberately bright light added a touch of surrealism to these inquisitions. She was merciless in her pursuit of evil, real or imagined, and when even the most resolute was reduced to tears, her mouth would stretch palely into what was almost a smile as she watched, unmoving and unmoved.

When Stella had stayed in her place in chapel on three consecutive Mass mornings, letting everyone else squeeze past her to go to the altar rails, Mother Michael sent for her to go to the white bathroom. I remembered Oona's remark about the Gestapo and feared for my friend. Stella was with her for a long time and when she crept back into the dormitory her face was pale and tired but I was glad to see that she hadn't been crying. I wanted to comfort her but remembered one day of savage recriminations when Mother Michael had found Patsy and Mary Clare holding hands and crying together over a horse which had been destroyed when it broke a leg jumping in Mrs Meredith's *manège,* and I was afraid: Stella was my dearest friend and I was too afraid to help her.

Inevitably news of Father Ryan's involvement in the accident percolated through the school: a newspaper cutting left in a desk; a clandestine whisper, forbidden but not unduly worried over by a day girl, who went home in the evening where the incident was just one of many others to be discussed over the family dinner-table, and by the time Stella returned we all knew who had killed her mother.

I was astonished to see Father Ryan celebrating Mass just three days later as if nothing had happened. I realised suddenly that it was to be as if nothing *had* happened, but I could hardly bear to look at him and I avoided all unnecessary contact with Ursula.

Was it that I was afraid that the words would spring, uncontrolled, from my mouth involving her in the misdeed? I think it was because I wanted to keep hidden until such time as I needed to use it, the knowledge I possessed of what she had done, that I had the power to hurt and destroy her; for my wickedness, which Mother Patrick had tried so hard to control, was not deeply buried but covered only lightly by ritual and expediency.

If Mother Michael had asked me directly about Ursula and Father Ryan I should have told her what I had seen, but the truth was only one casualty of this affair and I knew my secret would be left undisturbed. Father Ryan had gone to see the Bishop, had made his confession, received absolution and was free to continue ministering to the needs of one hundred and two adolescent girls.

Mrs Lightowler had stepped in front of his car in the dark and he couldn't avoid hitting her. In spite of a number of people walking home from a birthday party, PC Reece could find no witnesses, which was a relief both to him and his mother, with whom he lived, as he was an active member of the Knights of St Columba and she enjoyed a special status in the Union of Catholic Mothers.

We always had to keep silence until breakfast time and on the morning after Stella's cross examination by Mother Michael we stripped our beds and put on our black veils before joining the line outside the chapel without any of us being able to find out from Stella what had been said to her in the white bathroom. I was standing next to her and I thought how fatigued she looked. There were dark smudges under her eyes and her skin seemed as if it had been pulled too tightly over her bones, but she stood holding her missal, the usual quiet expression on her face.

Mother Michael came silently out from the shadow of an alcove, beyond which was the juniors' dormitory. I heard Stella draw in a long, shaky breath, but that was all. Mother Michael stopped beside us and I felt Stella's arm pressing against mine as we stood there and all I could do was to try to return the pressure without Mother Michael being aware of it.

The nun's voice was cold, each word like a little shard of ice.

'Stella Lightowler, you have not been to Holy Communion for a week and I do not expect you to abstain from taking Communion this morning. Surely you, of all people, should be partaking of the sacrament to offer it up for the release of your mother's soul from purgatory.'

Stella hadn't needed to tell me why she wouldn't go to Communion. As the threats and pressure of the night before in the white bathroom had not broken her resolution I could see that this was how Mother Michael was going to try now, by public humiliation.

Stella turned very slightly towards the nun and her voice was quite steady.

'I shan't be going to Communion, Mother Michael. Father Ryan killed my mother because he was drunk and I shall never take Communion from him again.'

Her voice flowed over all of us: down the curving stairs with the emerald glass banister, up to the glass dome, now covered with a lace cloth of frost, along the galleries to every empty bed, into the kitchens and Hall, music-rooms and library. It echoed along the still, dark corridors and came to rest at the feet of Father Ryan as he robed in his acid-green chasuble in the decadence of the pink marble sacristy.

For one suspended second I thought that Mother Michael was going to strike Stella but she leaned across me and the smell of her fasting-induced breath made me flinch, as she hissed,

'How dare you say such a thing about a man who is a priest of God, how dare you, Stella Lightowler. I haven't finished with you yet. Oh no!'

She said very sharply to the two youngest girls at the front of the line, 'Lead into chapel.'

And as Mother Michael moved to open the door Regina, who was standing behind us, murmured,

'I shall not go to Communion today,' and I heard, 'Nor me, nor me,' echoing, whispered, down the line.

By the time the consecration bell rang I was so afraid of what we were doing that I didn't feel as if I could have walked to the altar rails. The younger girls went first: left-hand pew, right-hand pew, down the outside aisle and back to their places through the rows of nuns, each one kneeling at her high prie-dieu.

It was just as well that it was Regina who was in the end seat of our row for when she should have led us along the blue carpet between the kneeling girls, she sat up just as she had said she would and all of us who were Stella's friends followed her example. With one exception. Ursula, composed and graceful, left her seat and walked slowly forward, her hands clasped in front of her and her eyes on Father Ryan, entangled too tightly in a net of lies and lust and complicity to risk any departure from the ordinary.

Reverend Mother's head was bowed and covered by her veil which was pulled forward over her face, but something of the atmosphere in the chapel must have penetrated even her withdrawal and she lifted back the veil with her long white hands and considered carefully the girls sitting in two quiet, defiant rows.

It was she that morning, not Mother Michael, who stood outside the door and to whom we curtsied as we left the chapel. As each of Stella's friends passed her, she looked straight into their eyes and

I felt again the way I had when she had instructed Caro and me all those years ago, and I knew that we were safe.

We were all punished, of course, for disrespect to God and disobedience of the rules and we had to sweep and polish the classrooms and wash the supper dishes for a week in the little auxiliary kitchen next to the dining-room, but it was a gentle punishment and much less than we expected. We had waited, uneasy, for the call to go to Mother Michael, but it never came. It was Mother Benedict who told us of our punishment and Mother Clare who supervised the execution of it.

A few days later a sulky Regina and I were sweeping out a room which overlooked the yard at the back of the house. It was a Saturday and the convent was emptier than usual and quiet, as the Junior teams had gone to play in a netball match at the other side of the county. Mother Clare had just made her rounds and Regina walked over to the window, dragging the big, soft brush behind her. She turned round quickly, her face animated.

'Quick, Isobel, come and look. What do you make of that?'

There was a taxi parked outside Father Ryan's front door and while we watched, he appeared carrying two very old suitcases, one tied round with rope. He put them on the ground and went back inside and then came out again carrying a tartan holdall and wearing his short black raincoat and a black hat. He was smoking a cigarette and we saw the taxi driver put all the luggage into the boot of his car and Father Ryan throw down his cigarette. He ground it into the cobbles of the yard then pulled the door of the cottage to and closed it very gently. Neither man spoke and the car slid quietly out of the yard.

'Well, well,' said Regina, 'I should think so too. I wonder how they'll explain *that* to the parents, just say he was ill, I suppose.' She turned to me.

'The only person who'll miss him is that creepy cousin of yours, wouldn't you say?'

I was alarmed. Regina always seemed to know so much about everyone that I did wonder how much she guessed about Ursula's and Father Ryan's conspiracy, so I didn't look at her and just muttered something about wondering who would take over from him now.

She looked at me with the mocking expression she often seemed to wear when talking to me. Suddenly I longed to be with Jack: to be by the sea and to talk to him of the nuns' duplicity and not to have to try to explain what I couldn't fully understand myself. The feeling was so intense that for a moment I felt dizzy and had to put my hand on one of the desks as I thought that I was going to fall over. Regina looked concerned.

'Oh come on, Isobel, we've done enough. Clarabelle's already been in here and she won't come back. Let's go and tell the others about Father Ryan.'

Patsy and Carmel had the worst of all jobs. They were dusting the scrolls and flowers entwined along the bronze railings that edged the curving stairs from the main hall to the top landing. Regina and I fetched two very clean and ironed blue-checked dusters and started to work downwards toward them. Mother Benedict was sitting in the hall reading her Office so we had to whisper our news of the priest's departure.

Canon Murchison, who was old and fat and wheezy and who lived in a flat attached to the old convent, took Benediction that evening. He was retired and acted as locum for all the priests in the surrounding parishes. No reason was ever given to explain Father Ryan's defection, we were told only that he had been called away on personal business and that the canon would be standing in for him until the end of term.

I was wondering how I was going to manage to avoid Ursula during the Christmas holidays at home. The holiday wasn't long enough for us to go to Cornwall and, besides, my mother set great store by a family Christmas and we would all be together for four weeks in that small house, trying to hold on to a spirit of goodwill that was as fleeting as it was false.

I decided that the only thing I could do was to pretend that none of it had ever happened; it meant that for the time being Ursula had won but I wouldn't allow myself even to think about Mrs Lightowler or Father Ryan and I pushed Mother Michael into the recesses of my mind until fear of what I knew surfaced and nibbled away at the edges of my thoughts and then I forced myself to imagine that I was sitting on the turf above an azure sea and that the sun was shining, and I made myself feel the happiness that I could only now imagine.

12

After the frosty beauty of the country London seemed like a grey well of coldness. It was already beginning to get dark when we reached Waterloo and coloured lights were spangling the streets but there was a taste of sulphur in the air and I missed, with an abrupt astonishment, the fields and hedges which surrounded us for most of the year.

Winter was my favourite season; I liked to see the bare bones of the trees standing around the edges of the ploughed fields, frosted old man's beard lying like snow along the hawthorn bushes with their scarlet berries bravely shining right to the end of winter.

Once when I had been staying with Antonia we had climbed the hill behind her grandmother's house and sat on a fallen tree trunk to look down on a flooded field where swans were swimming far below us in a lake spilled from the broken banks of the river, and as we watched, the hounds were led out for their daily trot along lanes which divided the countryside into pieces like a puzzle and which only on bare winter days showed sections fitted together to make a whole.

Winter gave you a chance to see into secret

places; lighted rooms at dusk before the curtains were drawn and houses where a tree obscured the view became ordinary when seen without an arcane veil of greenery, but the privet hedges and plane trees of London were black with grime and the dead heads of buddleia, which seemed to grow out of every precarious crevice on the bomb sites, nodded towards clumps of Michaelmas daisies and decaying Valerian.

Ursula, Caro and I walked over the long, echoing footbridge to catch the train to London Bridge Station, where we changed to the suburban line. From this train you could see tall, terraced houses beside the track, their yellow bricks blotched with soot. Their windows were on a level with the carriages and through net curtains there were tableaux of Christmas trees in corners and paper decorations, little oblong peepshows of yellow light, as the train rumbled past.

There were window-boxes where straggly plants were all that were left of the summer's ambitions and some of the houses had a kitchen built on at the back where old baths and treadle sewing-machines, bicycles and rabbit hutches grew in the murky gardens. Here and there was a space where a house had stood before the bombing and weeds and grass traced where flower beds had been. Occasionally still there was half a house waiting for demolition, with a fireplace hanging on a bedroom wall and where faded wallpaper unpeeled slowly like bark from a silver birch.

Christmas with Frank and my mother was like

walking through quicksand. There *was* a path and if you found it and walked steadily along you eventually came on to firm ground some time after the New Year.

My mother tried so hard but a week wasn't long enough for a foundation of trust to be laid anew and we spent so little time at home that each holiday was a new beginning. We were strangers, but with true strangers there would have been no memory of broken promises and indifference.

Ursula was the only one of us who seemed able to negotiate the hazards with impunity. I watched as she laughed at my mother's pitiless impersonations of her friends, treating her opinions as if they were jokes and telling my mother how clever she was, how observant and amusing.

There were three parcels from America in the dining-room; a very large one for Ursula and two smaller ones. Caro's and mine had been undone and rather untidily rewrapped. My mother, in answer to my question, said that they had obviously been opened by Customs and changed the subject.

We went to Midnight Mass, the ugly grey church transformed by candlelight and green boughs into a warm and joyous manifestation of hope. It was the best part of Christmas and I tried to concentrate the feeling so that I could carry some of it with me when we walked home through streets, iced and slippery, to whatever the day would bring.

Frank gave us all a Brownie Reflex camera and my mother had knitted each of us a new cardigan. We left the American parcels until last; Ursula's mother had sent Caro and me bright cotton scarves and little brooches of ladybirds and frogs set with sparkly stones. Ursula's present was a short fur coat, as white and warm as down. She put it on, pulled the collar up round her ears and nestled instinctively into its softness: it was quite extraordinary but she looked absolutely sweet and innocent. There was an American sweater for her in the parcel, of palest-yellow angora with seed pearls scattered over the yoke, and nylon stockings and a bracelet.

Caro and I had bought our mother a large bottle of bright-pink bath salts at the Christmas Bazaar and as soon as she unwrapped them I knew that we had made a mistake.

'Thank you,' she said and put them down beside her chair as I heard her mutter to Frank, 'They smell like cat's pee.' It was enough, and by the time Bill and Babs arrived in the middle of the morning her mood was becoming dangerous.

They gave us money and for my mother and Frank there was a large box of chocolates. Frank and Bill exchanged bottles and my mother handed Babs a flat parcel: inside it were four pairs of nylons.

'Oh,' I said, 'how funny, they're the same brand as Ursula got from America. Isn't that a coincidence?'

'*What* a coincidence,' my mother said, her voice as smooth as cream.

She didn't speak to me for the rest of the day. Not a word; it was as if I'd become invisible, and much later when Bill and Frank were doing the washing up together and we were playing Monopoly on the dining-room table we heard raised voices in the sitting-room.

'You're a bit hard on her, Iris. She didn't realise you'd filched them from their parcels.'

'Oh, of course she knew. She just said it to embarrass me. You don't know her, Babs, she did it to ruin my Christmas and she succeeded, little bitch. Trust her to spoil everything, just like her bloody father.'

'Well, I think you're making a mountain out of a molehill, it's only some nylons, for God's sake.'

'I see, so nylons aren't good enough for Mrs Bill Rocastle now that she's so rich and lives in a big house in a classy road. You forget that I knew you when you'd have done anything for a pair of nylons — and did too, I remember. And another thing, you can take back your chocolates, I suppose a client gave them to Bill and you thought of your poor relations.'

My mother's voice was loud, embittered by disappointment and too many gins. Babs and Bill had moved in the summer to an outer suburb where they had a big house and an acre of garden. My mother's jealousy was relentless. I listened, saddened, as I knew this was the prelude to the breakdown of another friendship. I'd seen it happen so often.

'If that's what you think, Iris, I'll give you something else to think about. Frank could have done just as well as Bill, God knows we gave him every opportunity, so ask yourself why he hasn't. What's held him back?

'Bill bought that house dirt cheap and you know it but when he offered one to Frank, who was it who said she wasn't prepared to live in a slum? If you didn't have the vision to see what could have been, then don't blame other people who had and who took that chance.'

There was silence and I imagined my mother biting her lip in that characteristic way she had. I had kept the wrapping paper from America to cut off the stamps and when I fetched it and looked at the Customs declaration I could see that part of it had been clumsily scratched out.

'You should learn to keep your mouth shut, Bel.'

Caro passed the dice to Ursula, who moved the Top Hat past GO and said, 'She didn't realise, Caro, she's not as devious as us, you know. Two hundred pounds please.' She smiled at me and for a moment I almost liked her. But only for a moment.

Ursula was right: I hadn't understood what my careless words were unleashing but I was just beginning to understand that I was only the catalyst by which my mother's moods were changed from light to dark, from generosity to savagery, in the twinkling of an eye.

It was a fearsome tightrope to walk, to keep not only my own balance but the whole equilibrium of the family, Frank and Caro being caught and held in the spreading tendrils of her unhappiness when she had finished with me. Frank did anything to appease her and Caro and I despised his weakness. It was only Ursula smiling that impenetrable smile who was left unscathed and I could see that sometimes she deliberately drew the scent away from me, and for that I was grateful.

Some while later my mother left the sitting-room without a word and it wasn't until Bill and Babs were leaving that anyone thought to look for her. She was fast asleep, Bab's new fur coat lying next to her like a great hairy body on Frank's side of the bed.

I was waiting for everyone to settle down so that I could lock myself in the lavatory. There was a key in the bathroom door but half of the door was made of frosted glass and it was only in the lavatory that we could be sure of privacy. I had kept my grandmother's letter in my pocket all day, managing to open it when attention was focused on Ursula's spectacular coat.

I had put the card with a £5 note inside it on my pile of presents, folded the envelope and slipped it into my pocket before I thought anyone had seen the letter it enclosed.

I had read Jack's letter twice during the day but I wanted to read it again, trying to conjure his voice through the paper and ink. My grandmother had sent on to me all the letters Jack had written while he was away in the army. Her handwriting was known at school and her letters were not opened and censored, the only difficulty was in finding somewhere to hide them from the nuns. I had a photograph of my mother and Frank on their wedding day on my bedside locker and I prised the back off this and slid Jack's letters behind the picture.

I had to find somewhere else at home though and hadn't yet thought of somewhere secure enough. My mother said it was her right to read my diary and short of wrestling it from her there was nothing I could do once she had found it, and I had to submit to the humiliation of hearing it read aloud to her friends. She did the same thing with the few letters I received, snatching them from my hands as soon as they arrived, but I was determined that Jack's letters would remain private.

His Christmas letter was very short but it told me what I wanted to know. His National Service was nearly finished and he would be home in the spring:

> The desert's beautiful in its own way but I long for some Cornish rain and the sound of the sea. I shall be home at Easter and you must come down — your grandmother will arrange something — and we'll go to St Just, just to make sure it's still there!

I put the letter in my dressing-gown pocket and, as quietly as I could, unlocked the lavatory door and started to walk towards my bedroom.

Ursula must have been listening because she opened her door and called softly, 'Isobel! Come in here a minute.'

Her room smelled powdery and delicious and she closed the door behind me.

'Look, I'm sorry about today, it really wasn't your fault.'

'I know that but if it hadn't been the stockings it would have been something else, so there's nothing to say.'

'That isn't what I wanted to say actually. It's about the letter you've been hiding all day.'

How did she know about it, I had been so careful. I could feel myself blushing and hoped she didn't notice in the dim light from the lamp beside her bed. My hand closed over the papers in my pocket.

'It's easy enough to hide things behind photos at school so why don't you do the same thing here? Aunty Iris isn't so keen on housework that she'll take down pictures to dust them and there are plenty of places to choose from.'

I must have looked taken aback because she laughed very quietly. 'Everyone does it, didn't you know? It's usually photos of boyfriends but you can use it for any kind of message as long as you have an understanding with someone else.'

A sudden picture came into my mind of Sister Gabriel, flustered and clumsy, replacing a picture of the Infant of Prague that she was dusting in the long corridor. I wondered why Ursula was telling me this and I wished desperately that she wasn't. I didn't want to know more about her than I already did, for I knew such knowledge was too much of a liability.

‘Oh, don’t worry, I won’t read your letters but I thought I owed you a favour.’

That was all she said but we both knew what she meant and all too easily I entered into an alliance with her, to protect my secret. I wished I had told her that I didn’t need her favours, but the moment when I could have done so passed and I opened the door of her bedroom and crossed the landing into the orange-smelling darkness of the room I shared with Caro, and when I was sure that she was asleep I used my nail file to force open the back of a long, black-framed photograph of Frank’s old school and manoeuvred Jack’s letters inside.

I lay awake for a long time, thinking about Jack in the desert and my grandmother alone, except for Sonja, in the big old house by the sea. The wish to be there with her was like a physical pain and tears of self-pity pricked my eyes. Before I went to sleep I got up again and took Jack’s letters out of their hiding place. I slipped them under the carpet, repositioning the old blanket chest that Caro and I had used as a toy box. I didn’t trust Ursula that much.

I thought, too, of something she had said when I was looking at the defaced Customs slip.

‘You should learn to question things a bit more, Bel, you’re so naïve. You should ask your friend Regina to tell you a few of the facts of life some time.’

‘What do you mean?’

‘Well, why do you think she was sent all the

way to England to school when there are perfectly good convents in Bogota or Bombay or wherever her father is now?'

'A lot of girls are sent here, why should there be anything funny about that?'

'Oh Isobel! That's what I mean about believing everything you're told. You ask her about the boy-friend her mother had just before Regina was sent away. How do you think she knows so much about men and sex? Just ask her, you might learn a lot from her.'

I suspected that what Ursula said was true. Regina had always been different from the rest of us but how did Ursula know so much about her? Regina detested her and I felt sure that she wouldn't have told her anything. But Ursula knew about my letters and I wondered what other secrets she kept hidden behind those long, chocolate eyes.

I determined not to let down my guard although she seemed to be doing her best to be agreeable to me and, reluctant as I was to admit it, I was beginning to understand the attraction she exerted. I resented too the fact that even Caro sometimes took Ursula's side against me in an argument now.

Christmas passed but we still had to negotiate the New Year; the narrows lined with jagged rocks of malice, storm waves of jealousy all but drowning us when we went to Bill and Babs. Babs's vitality and generosity ensured that their party was the one everyone wanted to go to, trying to stall other invitations until hers arrived. We always went, of course, but this year I was one of the adults and in spite of my mother's attempts to discomfit me, I enjoyed myself. I was beginning to enjoy Babs's company altogether. She gave me some of her old face powder and a half-used Tangee lipstick and persuaded me to wear my long hair loose sometimes instead of tightly plaited.

'You're never going to be beautiful like Ursula, Isobel, but you've got something that she hasn't. Think of Lesley Caron and Zizi Jeanmaire, they're not what you'd call pretty, are they? It's what the French call gamine — but I think their style of looks is going to be in fashion and, anyway, your figure is much better than Ursula's — she's got hockey player's legs, haven't you noticed?'

I was immensely cheered by this although I couldn't really believe it, and Babs continued to be kind to me and took me to a matinee at Covent Garden to see Moira Shearer dancing in *Swan Lake*. Sometimes we went shopping and wandered around Selfridges and Swan and Edgar and I thought it glamorous and exciting to walk through the Burlington Arcade.

Strange shapes were appearing on the South Bank and London was full of anticipation of the Festival of Britain which the King and Queen were going to open at the beginning of May and there was a feeling of hopefulness, of good times so long delayed, having nearly arrived. Prettiness and colour were tiptoeing back into the drab spaces left by the war and a determination to be happy was everywhere.

Things were never quite the same after that silent Christmas. It was as if Bill and Babs, by distancing themselves physically from us, could see suddenly and clearly what was happening. My mother was always nicer to us when Babs was around and Babs seemed to enjoy having me as an occasional companion so there was an edgy truce between them and my mother found another confidante in a wrinkled, painted old woman who told us that she was a White Russian.

She looked like a monkey, a dirty monkey, and her thin hair was dyed the colour of carrots. She lived in a room on the ground floor of a very grand house which she hinted belonged to her nephew. On one wall was a looking-glass quite as large as the one we had in the ballet class and in this she made Caro and me stare at ourselves wearing jewel-encrusted ballgowns and floating chiffon dresses which she dragged out of an enormous wardrobe smelling of musty, long-dead roses, that essence of old ladies' bedrooms.

She stood very close to us and the rings on her fingers flashed as she ran her hands down the front of our bodices and when we flinched away in embarrassment, she would look at us with those simian eyes and smile at the reflections in the glass.

While we changed back into our sensible skirts and jerseys she would watch us, sitting on the stool of her dressing-table and then she would give us something from the drawer in front of her; a comb, a small leather notebook, a brooch, all grubby and covered in hair and spilled powder. We always threw them away as soon as we got home.

Our mother sat on a spindly gold chair watching all this as if it were a play and when we sulked and said that we didn't want to go there any more, she told us we were silly girls and if we had played our cards right we might have been given something decent after a while.

It was Frank who unwittingly rescued us from this ordeal. He had lunched with Bill in a pub near the house where my mother's new friend lived, and Bill had pointed out to him the odd little figure sitting at one end of the bar.

'She lives next door to the house we were in this morning, tells everyone her nephew owns it! She reckons she's a White Russian but after one or two she sounds more like Whitechapel to me. The chap who lives in the flat above her swears she was the Madam of a brothel. I had a look round when I was in there last week and she's got some good stuff but the whole place gave me the creeps, I didn't hang around.'

As soon as he started telling us this story over supper one night, we realised that Frank was talking about our mother's friend and it was only Caro pressing hard on my foot that stopped me blurting out that we sometimes went to visit her and that we hated her because she made us try on her old clothes. I looked covertly at my mother, wondering what she would do. She gave no indication whatever of knowing what Frank was talking about and just laughed and said, 'Trust Bill to go brothel-creeping,' but we were never taken there again.

My mother had a succession of odd friends. There was a family of Polish refugees; two sisters, a husband, a son, but whose husband, whose son, was never made clear: a war widow who lived at the bottom of the road and whose son, the same age as Caro, shrieked and dribbled, soaking the front of his clothes as he stood and rattled at the gate: a tall, handsome bachelor we met in church every Sunday who blushed and mumbled and who was dropped precipitately when Ursula and Caro, giggling, reported seeing him in the park one evening with a friend.

We didn't have many friends of our own in London. When we came home for the holidays we were isolated by education and convention and had to rely on each other for company. The parish priest introduced us to the Youth Club but when we tried to join in we found that spontaneity dried up; we embarrassed them and we heard laughter and exaggerated mimicry of our voices when the swing doors closed behind us.

Our real lives still had their centre in Cornwall, in the small rough places of West Penwith with its soft rains, where sudden squalls rushed across the fields, flattening the barley and reminding your mouth of the taste of the sea. Grey stone hedges shielded fields of daffodils and anemones, which we helped to bunch on the kitchen table at the farm, wrapping raffia carefully around the stems and laying bunches of a dozen flowers in shallow cardboard boxes. Sometimes there were violets, the colour of a Cadbury's wrapper, and we picked these with fingers numb from the cold and the dew.

The years we had spent in London intensified our longing to be back there; to see tiny bananas growing, hidden in ragged, bright-green leaves; where blue and pink hydrangeas nodded to each other like gossips over each whitewashed wall in the steep, grey town where every road led to the sea and children used the high-walled back lanes as their secret roads and where St Michael guarded our lives from his fastness in the bay.

13

The year that followed the Festival of Britain was the last we were ever to spend all together as Ursula was going to leave school at the end of the summer term. She was going to fly out to her mother in Los Angeles, where her beautiful face and her steely determination would prove to serve her as well as any academic qualifications, because of those she would have few.

Other people were beginning to understand what I had always known, that Ursula was not really clever at all. It was only when she had to write down the answers in an examination that the measure of her lack of knowledge became apparent. Usually by transposing any question she was somehow able to convey that she had answered and if someone pressed her further she would look at them, smiling and slightly puzzled as to why they persisted. It was nearly always successful and to those who didn't know her well, it seemed as if she withheld knowledge in a deliberate effort to appear unassuming.

She had memorised several quotations, sufficiently abstruse for her to be able to explain the meaning to anyone who showed an interest, and she knew thoroughly the intricacies of one or two pieces of music and would hum 'Pavane for a Dead Infanta' once she had introduced it into the conversation. She could distinguish Monet and Manet sufficiently to confound anyone not already confused, and in this way she spread a small knowledge far enough to hoodwink many people into believing that she was a good deal cleverer than she really was.

From almost the beginning of our acquaintance I was aware of something missing in Ursula, some element of normality absent, which I didn't understand at all until we grew older and I was always surprised that other people seemed unaware of it, as it seemed so obvious to me. They accepted Ursula at her own valuation, which was high, and I knew instinctively that they were wrong to do so. I always felt that behind the enticing smile and distancing manner there was something very dangerous, made more so by the fact that Ursula herself seemed unaware of it.

She was certainly conscious of the effect she had on people and manipulative in her self-interest but it seemed to me that this knowledge was limited, as if the surface reaction was all she was interested in. Having lit the blue touch-paper she retired and seemed indifferent to whatever fireworks she had set off. In this way she was able to detach herself from the consequences of her actions — and that was where the danger lay.

I don't believe, in all the years we spent in such intimacy, that I ever really saw Ursula relax: every gesture, every expression seemed calculated, each word and action governed by a will-power that never slackened or slipped into unconstrained enthusiasm or genuine excitement. She played with people's feelings in an alarmingly offhand way yet her own emotions were kept under such tight control that I wondered many times if she really felt anything at all.

That summer, that hot sepia summer, Ursula's loveliness was startling. She had always been more than just pretty but now the promise was nearly fulfilled and each time you looked at her your eyes acknowledged the advent of great beauty. She was so unlike the rest of us that jealousy was never part of that recognition and even I was able to appreciate in a detached way what I was watching. Mother Benedict hovered and gloated, her protégée to be guarded like some rare flower from the greenhouse brought out into the open air to be accustomed to the harsher climate of the garden before being displayed as the centrepiece of some public exhibition.

As Ursula blossomed in that far-off summer, so little Sister Gabriel seemed overtaken by some unspecified ailment. Her pallor and lassitude were obvious even to the unobservant and sometimes she would be sent with a message, only to forget the content and would stand with her blue eyes filling with tears before hurrying away.

She had always seemed to occupy a space half-way between the Community and us, so young and friendly compared with the rest of the nuns that we sometimes almost forgot that the same rules which applied to their lives, applied also to hers. She was so ingenuous and unsophisticated that I imagine her access to our conversations and the fact that many of us accepted her presence, indeed hardly noticing that she was there, was of great use to anyone unscrupulous enough to use it.

We asked Mother Clare if Sister Gabriel were ill and she told us that she was suffering from a 'crisis of faith' and as soon as the term ended she would be going back to the Mother House for a period of rest and the re-examination of her vows. She was rather tired but there was nothing for us to concern ourselves about although we should, of course, pray for her.

There was plenty to occupy our minds other than Sister Gabriel. Reverend Mother General was making a Visitation of the sister houses and Mother Michael was implacably determined that Stella Maris would become the flagship of the English convents. Stella Maris, only four years into its experiment with exclusively senior education and hampered by its role as a finishing school for girls from abroad, was to outshine Regina Coeli and Fidelis and the only way to do this was to excel in every department. The fact that we had only half as many girls as the other two convents meant that we had to work twice as hard and then a little more to show what we had achieved, driven by Mother Michael's compulsion to succeed.

Reverend Mother General's visit was at the beginning of June just before the examinations which were supposed to determine the direction our lives would take, but it was considered far more important. If anyone really wanted to work, the best hospitals would accept Stella Maris girls for training as nurses and so would the secretarial colleges in the fashionable area of London between Berkeley Square and Farm Street. Few, though, had ambitions beyond filling in the time between school and marriage. By far the largest number would stay at home helping their mothers or making themselves useful with the horses and laying the foundations of a lifetime's social network; most, sooner or later, finding a husband. It was obvious that the Visitation should take precedence over examinations.

Mother Michael was determined to achieve perfection: those to whom perfection was a distant prospect she bullied and cajoled, terrified, punished and, occasionally, praised, until no more could be wrung out of anyone. When that point was reached she renewed her striving to improve on the best that had already been achieved and from somewhere we found the reserves to continue. We hated her for it but in the years that followed I wondered if we misjudged her, if the strength we found in times of adversity stemmed from defying Mother Michael's censure.

Ursula and I were to lead the dancing display but she alone was to make the welcoming speech, her poise and reliable-enough French enabling Mother Benedict to persuade Reverend Mother that Ursula was the obvious choice although we all agreed that it should have been Esther Rainbird, who was now Head Girl.

The Visitation was to start officially with Mass on Monday morning and we were given a free Sunday afternoon, forbidden in fact to rehearse or practise any more, and there was cake for tea and butter instead of the usual pale, thick margerine to spread on our bread.

Stella and I decided to use our free afternoon to go and pick wild strawberries where we knew they were growing, soft and luscious, on the banks of a wood where the trees had been thinned to saplings. Stella had the leading role in the play we had been rehearsing for weeks, a performance which would be repeated at the end of term on Parents' Day and to which Stella's father would have to come on his own for the first time.

I thought back to one Easter, when we had sung Pergolesi's *Stabat Mater* and how Mother Michael had sent for me on the morning of the concert.

'Come in, Isobel, I have a job I want you to do for me.'

She was holding a pile of small white cards and on each was written in Mother Clare's clear italic script the name of one of the guests for the evening's concert.

'This is a task that requires tact and discretion and I am giving it to you as I know that I can rely on your common sense to see that it is carried out properly. You are to place these cards on the seats of the chairs in the Hall, keeping family members together but bearing in mind, please, that we do not want, for instance, Mr and Mrs Lightowler to be seated next to Lady Fairfax-May — it would be uncomfortable for all of them. I am sure that you understand what I am saying, Isobel?'

And I had gone away and divided the sheep from the goats and had felt faintly tainted ever since.

In the months following her mother's death, Stella and I had grown very close. We had so far managed to conceal the depth of our friendship from Mother Michael as she would certainly have done her best to separate us. Antonia was my closest friend but Stella and I had something in common which we shared with no one: we alone knew the true depth of Ursula's perfidy and between us we kept that knowledge hidden but alive. It bound us together in a way that nothing else could have done and was as pernicious as anything else that Ursula was ever responsible for.

The woods were cool and quiet, soft underfoot and dark. The syringa was in flower again but in the closeness of the trees that overpowering smell was diminished and we walked silently for most of the time, the sunlight patchy where it broke through the leaves overhead.

The strawberries were at the far end of the wood and as we walked in Indian file along a path bordered by uncurling bracken, something moving in a thicket to our right caught Stella's eye and thinking it might be a deer she stopped so suddenly that I bumped into her. She put her hand on my arm and whispered, 'Shush.'

It wasn't a deer. Ursula was sitting on the ground with Sister Gabriel, their arms around each other and even as we watched, Ursula leaned forward and kissed the young nun on the mouth. They obviously hadn't heard us and we were able to turn and walk quickly and silently away along the yielding path, wild strawberries blotted from our minds. I was shaking as if I were freezing and I couldn't look at Stella. I understood the implication of what we had seen although I tried not to think about it by concentrating on the colour of the ferns brushing against my legs, the shape of the newly emerged fronds, anything, rather than Ursula's brown arms and Sister Gabriel's closed eyes.

We ran the last few yards through the trees, sunshine and shadows flickering around us, and threw ourselves down on a grassy bank in the shade of some myrtle bushes.

'What shall we do, Stella? We've got to tell someone but who's going to listen to us with RMG arriving this evening?'

Stella didn't seem to have heard me.

'Not even *her;* I wouldn't have believed it, not even of *her.*'

She obviously had heard me because she turned towards me. It was very warm and quiet in the shade of the myrtles; I could hear music coming faintly through an open window where someone was playing Chopin, the notes slow and clumsy, dropping into the silent afternoon. There was a grasshopper buzzing somewhere near us, and bees, but it was Stella's voice that I heard, even though she almost whispered the words.

'*No.* No, we won't tell anyone. We've got her now, Isobel: just where we want her, don't you *see?*'

I looked at Stella, knowing there was something wrong about the exultation in her voice. I knew what I was doing but denied my misgivings, even to myself, and agreed to say nothing about what we had seen in the bosky depths of the wood. Added to the dragging weight of apprehension of that knowledge there was something else worrying me much more.

Ever since her mother's death Stella had seemed to fade. She had always been quiet but it was quietness built on a foundation of confidence. If she had something to add to a conversation, she said it with the assurance of someone whose views had always been accepted as worthwhile, but she seldom chattered or took part in the giggling silliness that sometimes overtook the rest of us. The nuns had dissuaded her from talking about her mother's death; prayer and the accumulation of indulgences were supposed to counterbalance her need to keep her mother's memory alive until such time as she could truly accept the fact of her death.

We heard her weeping in the night but so strong was our fear of breaking Mother Michael's honour system that we turned away, abandoning her to keep our own conscience clear. I tried to help her, feeling that the death of my grandfather helped me to understand her grief. I was wrong, of course:

nothing could reach into the depths of bitterness she suffered, knowing that Father Ryan would never be called to account, and that the shattered lives of her family must be accepted as the will of God.

Now, in Stella's quiet, triumphant voice, I had heard revenge and I was uneasy. I thought about talking to Antonia but it seemed like a betrayal of Stella's trust and I felt that as long as we stuck together then nothing untoward would happen. How could I have understood?

We had the three days of the Visitation as grace and in the sunshine of the following afternoon Ursula and I stood at the head of two lines of girls in decorous net frocks while Sister Gudule did her best on the grand piano, hauled out on to the terrace for Reverend Mother General's visit. Ursula and I counted the beats while we waited to lead our lines out on to the parched grass where two evenings ago we had all knelt in a rebellious line, cutting with our nail-scissors the individual, stringy stalks of grass left behind by the mower.

I hated *Les Sylphides* and I hated Ursula but we had to go through those motions which would achieve Mother Michael's ambition, smiling and obedient as ever.

The inspections were finished, the displays and exhibitions dismantled; Esther had presented Reverend Mother General with a photograph of everyone at Stella Maris, preserved for ever one bright summer morning, chaste and virtuous in our Sunday dresses.

Reverend Mother General spoke to us in French and we laughed politely, taking our cue from the nuns. We clapped at her parting joke,

'Et maintenant, mes enfants, je vous dis, "bon acheter pour le cadeau".'

I tried to concentrate on work in the days that followed the Visitation, using all my will-power to clear my mind of the images that rose like a slide show behind my eyes. Sometimes, though, waves of panic swept over me and I felt transparent as if my foreboding and fear were visible like stems in a glass vase.

The routine of the convent returned to normal. Sister Gabriel continued to clean the long corridor once a week, taking down and dusting the engraving of the Infant of Prague as well as the pictures of St Anthony, and St Theresa holding a bunch of colourless flowers.

No one ever knew when it was that she had found the note left in Ursula's pre-arranged hiding place. Had she kept it close, reading and rereading the cruel, dismissive words while they festered in her mind or did they swiftly push, to the edge of endurance, reason already fragile; a spirit struggling to be free from the constriction of a Rule embraced far too young and now no longer tenable?

The note, pieces of which were later found, blotched and torn in the deep pocket of her habit, had been concealed behind the Infant of Prague who had always before been the guardian of tenderness and promise.

14

The hours at the beginning of the day were the only time I felt really free. From the time our door was opened with a 'Praised be Jesus Christ' and we answered with a muttered 'Amen', the day was structured to allow the devil no time for his work. I always woke early and enjoyed the luxury of lying still, allowing unformed thoughts to drift in and out of my mind, blurred or sharpened in my amorphous state.

I liked to know what the day was like before I had to venture out into it and from my bed next to the window one morning a little while after Reverend Mother General had left Stella Maris to go on to Fidelis, where the same dances would be danced and the same songs would be sung, and Reverend Mother General would make the same joke, I pulled the curtain aside, letting arcs of light drift on to my bed.

The dormitory overlooked the little lily pond, now covered in broad green leaves and surrounded by trimmed hedges which sheltered nymphs and naiads in arbours of green. There was a mist over the water, spreading its dusky fingers into all the still-unlit spaces of the small, secluded garden.

Gathered around the far edge of the pond was a group of figures, as grey and tenebrous as the vapour.

Mother Benedict, wearing her long, black cloak and a white nightcap, was holding one of the hooked wooden poles we used to open the art room windows. I pushed myself up in bed to see better but I knew already without needing visible proof: I knew it was Sister Gabriel, her soft white flesh dented by the brass hook as Mother Benedict pulled her slowly to the side where other hands reached out to hold her.

There was a pile of neatly folded clothes on the grass, the starched white bonnet lying on top of a faded-blue apron, black clogs side by side as if their owner had just gone for a little swim in the river of her childhood.

Mother Clare was holding Sister Gabriel's legs and she and Mother Benedict struggled to lift the small, pale body out of the water. Suddenly there was a splash, which I heard only in my imagination, and tall Mother Celestia dropped into the water, her white nightgown ballooning around her and the lily pads swaying in the ripples. She lifted Sister Gabriel clear of the edge before stepping out herself, a puddle forming around her wide, black feet. Reverend Mother unclipped her own cloak and laid it over the little nun, tucking it around her as tenderly as if she were putting a child to bed.

I saw the white of the ambulance intermittently as it came up the drive between hedges full of dog roses and cow parsley, but it was the sight of the shorn head, the hair so pitilessly short, lying on the golden flagstones and the luminous, pearly skin now prickled by the roughness of a black serge cloak that made me shiver as I dropped the corner of the curtain and sat back on my pillow. Stella was awake and watching me with such intensity that I felt as if the thoughts were being drawn out of my head and spun across the space between us and into her keeping.

She moved silently across the room and stood at the foot of my bed, still watching me as she pulled the edge of the curtain aside. The curtains were cream, quite plain, and edged with hand-crocheted lace and I remembered suddenly, with a pain that hurt my heart, Sister Gabriel sitting quietly in a corner while inches of the delicate work being woven by her small, rough hands coiled into the white cloth spread on her lap.

Stella and I watched as two ambulance men slid the body on to a stretcher and covered it with a blanket before carrying it out of our sight into the shadow of the house. We saw the ambulance drive away in the lightening morning, a hard, bright sun just beginning to colour the sky. Stella looked at me and smiled a small, ambiguous smile and walked back to her bed without a word. I remember very clearly that her pyjamas were the same soft pink as the wild roses.

There was no viewing of the body this time, no procession through the streets behind the hearse and no one from outside the convent was there when we sang a Requiem Mass for Sister Gabriel.

The smell of hay drying in ochre strips in the fields drifted in through the open chapel windows as I watched the smoke spiralling up from the altar candles once Sister Brigid had snuffed them out. I hoped that Reverend Mother was wrong when she had told us that suicides couldn't enter heaven and had to spend eternity in limbo with unbaptised babies and the heathen. Sister Gabriel didn't deserve that.

Reverend Mother looked again at the stained and crumpled letter that Mother Clare had brought her.

'Perhaps my knowledge of English is not as extensive as I had thought — I don't even understand some of these words and I won't embarrass you by asking you to explain them to me.' She touched a corner of the paper lightly, withdrawing her hand as if it burned. 'You believe this is true, Mother Clare?'

The younger nun nodded. 'I have no doubt, Reverend Mother.'

'I regret having to say so, but neither have I.' She got up and turned to look out of the window at a sky the colour of a bruise. 'It looks as though we shall have some rain at last.'

She didn't speak again for some minutes and Mother Clare standing quietly under a picture of the Pope wondered if she had been forgotten. It was terribly hot and her bonnet was making her face itch, the habit in summer was almost unbearable and many times a day she had to offer up her impatience and discomfort. Reverend Mother spoke again.

'I was just thinking about Mother Patrick. She *knew,* you know; all those years ago she warned me about Ursula but I didn't really understand and now I feel that I have failed her. It would never have come to this if I had been more vigilant.'

'We could all have been more vigilant, ma Mère. I certainly knew that Ursula needed to be watched. But Sister Gabriel; that's what's so hard to accept.'

'Sister Gabriel was ill, Mother, and it is not for us to judge her, but Ursula will have to be withdrawn at once, of course. I'll talk to her and then she is to be isolated in the Sanatorium until her uncle and aunt can arrange to fetch her. Will you send Matron to me and then find Ursula and wait with her until I am ready to talk to her. She is not to be allowed to mix with anyone and she will need to be made aware of the terrible nature of the sin she has committed. I, myself, must try to ensure that she does.'

Mother Clare knew that Ursula would be in the Common Room where we all sat on Saturday mornings while we mended our clothes or knitted layettes and blankets to be sent to the missions. We were listening to Mother Celestia reading to us from *The Flight of the Falcon* but I could think only that for every Saturday morning since I could remember, it had been Sister Gabriel who had sat in a corner while we were allowed to listen to the wireless and talk quietly.

It was stifling and so humid that morning that the pale-blue wool I was turning into a matinee jacket for the Black Babies Mission stuck to my fingers and I gritted my teeth as I had to drag the stitches along the sticky needle. Mother Celestia had a line of sweat on her upper lip and once or twice she had taken off her gold-rimmed glasses and wiped her face with her damp handkerchief. I felt sorry for her and thought longingly of the sea, and I knew that soon we would be in Cornwall again and Jack and I would sit on the cliffs at St Just and the breeze off the water would be cool; I felt better just imagining it. Mother Celestia closed the book.

'It's too hot for all of us in here today; I think there's going to be a thunderstorm so you'd better put away your work and go quietly outside for a little while to get some fresh air.'

Just as she spoke, the first lightning flashed over the horizon and we jostled each other out of the side door to the yard.

'Isobel, Ursula, just a moment, please.' Mother Clare was hurrying along the corridor, her fingers pushing the goffered edges of her bonnet away from her face. 'Reverend Mother would like to see you. Go along to Mother Michael's study, Isobel. I'll follow with Ursula.'

I heard the first heavy drops of rain falling on the corrugated-iron roof of the lean-to which covered the dustbins outside the back door. The heat which had been building up since yesterday was dissipated quite suddenly by the storm and I shivered.

Reverend Mother was sitting at Mother Michael's desk and Mother Michael herself stood beside the window. I couldn't see either nun's face against the light; the only face I saw clearly was Stella's and that was in my imagination, smiling again that curious, victorious smile she had given me as we had watched Sister Gabriel being taken away in the pale, morning mist.

There was a plain wooden cross on the desk and the letter lay beside it. I tried not to look at it, concentrating on Reverend Mother's hands which were folded in front of her. They had the same bony stillness as the praying hands in Dürer's drawing. Reverend Mother seemed reluctant to speak and I stood watching the rain streaming down the window-panes; the glass appeared to be melting.

'Isobel, I am sorry to have to ask you this, but have you at any time suspected that your cousin was,' a long pause, 'meeting Sister Gabriel? Please answer truthfully, you have nothing to fear.'

I felt Mother Michael's cold grey eyes on me and I, who had never dared to lie to her, thought of how much I hated Ursula and of how she had been responsible for so much of my unhappiness. I thought of Stella's mother and how Ursula had usurped my place with my own mother and I looked at the nun in front of me and said, 'No, Reverend Mother, I had no idea.'

She slid the incriminating note towards me, her

hand covering most of the words which I knew so well by heart.

'Is this Ursula's handwriting, Isobel?'

I looked at the signature, so carefully worked at and copied.

'I think so, Reverend Mother. Yes, I'm sure really.'

She pulled the paper back and half turned to Mother Michael, who spoke for the first time.

'I have telephoned your parents, Isobel, and your stepfather will be coming down tomorrow to take Ursula home. I, we, believe it would be better if you and Caroline were not to see him on this occasion and I have suggested that Ursula is sent out to her mother in the United States straight away, before you and your sister go home for the holidays. I am sure that I need not tell you that what has been spoken of here today is *never* to be repeated to anyone. Go back to your work now.'

I curtsied to Reverend Mother and when I opened the study door, there was Ursula sitting on one of the hard chairs that Sister Gabriel had polished every week, with Mother Clare next to her, her head bent to avoid my eyes.

Ursula looked at me with an expression on her face that I shall never forget. It was as if all the sadness and unfairness of our lives was, just for once, manifested and acknowledged. Ursula's dark eyes were full of understanding, but there was something else as well. It was as if her voice said quite clearly to me, 'You will have to carry this for ever now and by accepting the blame, I am transferring the burden to you.'

I half expected Mother Clare to have heard what Ursula had said but she stood up and motioned my cousin forward without looking at me. I understood at once and for ever that in destroying Ursula we had destroyed far more of ourselves.

Perhaps my mother and Frank had always been aware of the risks surrounding Ursula but they had never shared their thoughts with us. When we went home for the summer Caro's things had been moved into the bedroom that Ursula had used and we soon understood that she was not to be mentioned, ever.

Although she was no longer a physical presence, Ursula was always a shadow in our lives but in some hidden way which I still could not understand. It wasn't until my mother died that I began to see what Ursula had really meant to her.

My mother outlived Frank by several years. He was, as Mrs Rainbird had said, a good man, and he looked after my mother, trying to restrain her wilder excesses, derided and disregarded for doing so but patient in his Christian duty, and when he died it was as if her body, deprived of someone else to goad and drive, turned on itself instead and she became bent and twisted; the terrible pain accompanying this metamorphosis she bore with stoic fortitude.

Caro and I went together to clear out the house in South London where it was one of the few in the street not to have been turned into flats. Small black children were playing in gardens where years before Caro and I had been forbidden to visit and in that grey street, doors and window-frames were painted sunshine-yellow and bright-pink or blue, the colour of a Caribbean sea. Music came from transistor radios where young men peered under the bonnets of old cars: the secret suburban façade had gone for ever.

Caro was recently engaged and happy to be able to use the furniture from the house but I didn't want anything except a picture; it was the first thing I could remember being aware of as a small child. It had hung on the wall of the dining-room of our house in Cornwall and I associated it in some way with my father.

We were folding clothes and packing them into suitcases when I pulled open one of the drawers in the polished walnut dressing-table. In it was a book, an old ledger of Frank's from which the used leaves had been torn, and I saw that page after page was pasted with articles cut from newspapers and magazines with headlines like *Ursula Hosier, Bright New Star in the Hollywood Firmament*; and *English Rose takes Film City by Storm.*

I couldn't say anything but held the book out to Caro and, sitting side by side on the bed, just as we had slept together on the mattress on the floor of the flat so long ago, we looked at Ursula's image, cajoling, flirtatious, bewitching, rebuffing; ten years of her life captured in fading photographs and columns of extravagant words. My mother's vicarious life was all there, preserved in heart-breaking secrecy as if waiting for us to find it and pronounce absolution over it.

We never saw Ursula again, except on celluloid and in the gossip pages of magazines, where that soft, beautiful face smiled its empty, siren smile and the long, chocolaty eyes concealed their secrets still.

15

1973

It was getting cold in the evenings, darkness coming earlier as the sun flashed its last green stripe across the sky, the green that only those who watched every day knew as a secret sign of impending night.

I decided to light the fire for the first time that autumn and went to look for kindling and newspaper. There was a bundle of papers on the kitchen table which I had gathered up from around the house and put ready for Jack to collect when he passed on the way home to his white house on the cliff; I think he was experimenting with paper bricks to use as fuel at that time. I sorted idly through the papers, always finding something more to read.

It was a small paragraph in the *Western Morning News* that jumped out at me and as I leaned against the table I wondered how I could have missed it.

SUDDEN DEATH OF FILM STAR NUN

Ex-film starlet Ursula Hosier, 40, was found dead yesterday at the Stella Maris Convent, where she had formerly been a pupil, and where for several years she had been teaching speech and drama. In the 1950s Ursula Hosier was often compared to Rita Hayworth and had looked set for worldwide stardom but in 1963 she turned her back on Hollywood to become a nun and entered the convent, where she was known as Mother Veronica. During her schooldays at Stella Maris there had been a mysterious incident involving the suicide of a young sister, found drowned in a lily pond. Although never directly linked to it, rumours of her involvement pursued Ursula Hosier for many years.

My heart was hammering as I realised what those words I had so nearly missed meant. We were free at last, as the only other person in the world who had ever known who had written the note that Sister Gabriel had found was dead.

I looked at the date on the newspaper, it was five days old and I wondered why I hadn't seen it before. Then I remembered I had found it pushed under the sofa. I thought I understood and smiled as I tore it into strips which I laid in the fireplace and covered with kindling wood before lighting the fire which destroyed it for ever.

I decided to go and start making tea as I liked the cottage to be warm and welcoming when Stella got home.

The employees of G.K. HALL hope you have enjoyed this Large Print book. All our Large Print titles are designed for easy reading, and all our books are made to last. Other G.K. Hall Large Print books are available at your library, through selected bookstores, or directly from us. For more information about current and upcoming titles, please call or mail your name and address to:

G.K. HALL
PO Box 159
Thorndike, Maine 04986
800/223-6121
207/948-2962